THE SORCERER OF THE WILDEEPS

Kai Ashante Wilson

A TOM DOHERTY ASSOCIATES BOOK

NEW YORK

THE SORCERER OF THE WILDEEPS

Copyright © 2015 by Kai Ashante Wilson

Cover art copyright © 2015 by Karla Ortiz

Edited by Carl Engle-Laird

A Tor.com Book

Published by Tom Doherty Associates, LLC

175 Fifth Avenue

New York, NY 10010

www.tor.com

Tor® is a registered trademark of Tom Doherty Associates, LLC.

ISBN 978-1-4668-9191-3 (e-book)

ISBN 978-0-7653-8524-6 (trade paperback)

First Edition: September 2015

For LeRoy Whitfield, who fell first,
though ten times the warrior I was then or ever will be

The Sorcerer of the Wildeeps

Dear Uncle, I am minded to respond as follows, now you tell me that, in striving to retain our provinces beyond the mountains, Imperial Daluz squanders resources and troops we had, given the recent eastern incursions, much better husband: *Let the whole ultramontane go.* Let us, moreover, manumit every Harudes slave, allowing them all, as each one so desires, to return to his snowbound home. Having read this, and greatly astonished, you will doubtless exclaim: Who then shall plough our fields, and build our cities; care for our trueborn sons, and bear the bastards of our lust? For these questions, too, Uncle, I have the answer: *Let us take whom we need from the Summer continent. The blacks of the northern coast are a peaceable and undefended peoples, the men sturdy, the women fine. Let us expand all our colonies there,* and begin to cut down and export the cedar forests of Philipium; take for ourselves the pearl beds at Merqerish, the copper mines of Santa Caela. Fear not to awaken the wrath of the mighty Kingdom of

Olorum, nor that of the gods of Ashé who protect it; for Great Olorum lies at the southern extreme of Summer, and if its coffers lack for bottoms, and soldiers number beyond count, still the Kingdom sleeps, and will never rouse itself over any act of ours so many thousands of miles to the north. . . .

from Albion the Younger to the Elder, *The White Letters*, vol. 3, ch. 18

First of Seven

The merchants and burdened camels went on ahead into the Station at Mother of Waters. The guardsmen waited outside. Tufts of rough grass broke from the parched earth, nothing else green nearby. Demane squinted at the oasis. Palm trees and lush growth surrounded the lake, dazzle reflecting from the steely surface. Just look at her, Mother of Waters; was anything in the world more beautiful—?

"Sorcerer," said the captain, tapping Demane's arm. He got out of the way. Tall and thin, Captain escorted the caravanmaster to the front of the gathered brothers.

Earthy and round, the little man hopped up on a rock. "Your choices, gentlemen." Master Suresh l'Merqerim broke it down for them: "Leave us; and join some other group of saltmen going straight back north. Do so, and you go home beggars. Three silver halfweights are what you'll get from me, and not a whoring penny more. But permit me to ask: Who here has balls? *That* man I invite to press on with us! Hard men will be required on the road down past Mother of Waters, when we come to the Wildeeps, and later reach the wide prairies north of the great lady herself, Olorum City. Such men of courage as are among you, *they* shall know a rich reward once we arrive in Olorum. Loot, and *more loot*, I say! A whole Goddamned fistful of silver full-weight coins. In Olorum, I shall open up a heavy bag. You will stick a greedy hand down into it, and grab out just as much silver as one fat filthy fist can hold."

Nor had the caravanmaster quite finished. "We stay in Mother of Waters only for one night: tonight. Tomorrow dawn, this caravan hits the fucking road again." Suresh really could stand to slow down on the cussing. While it was true that most brothers showed purer descent from that half of the mulatto north supposedly more blessed with brawn than brains, and for the merchants it was the other way around—brighter of complexion (and intellect?)—did it necessarily follow that one group deserved fine speech, while the other should get nasty words sprinkled on every single sentence? "You motherfuckers came here on our coin, our camels. And while you lot drink and whore tonight, we merchants must sell the salt, must empty the warehouses, must pack the goods, must swap the camels for burros. Therefore—right now—I need numbers for how many mean to press on with us. Tell Captain Isa your choice: you brave, you venturesome, you men who *are* men. And may God bless the cowardly cocksuckers we leave behind."

The caravanmaster hopped down. From a sack, he handed out fragments of a slab-of-salt that had broken in transit. Plentiful chunks, which brothers could trade in the Station for room, board, and vice, went around. On his one free night, Demane wanted only to spend what a later age would call "quality time," not to run around Mother of Waters rescuing fools from folly. But even leaving aside those brothers intent on browsing the black market or the prefelonious with contraband themselves to fence, the very wisest plans Demane heard his brothers making were nothing of the kind. You had wantons looking forward to boughten love, tipplers to some beverage called "that Demon," gamblers to the local bloodsports... The guardsmen grinned and said *Thanky* as their cupped hands were filled to brimming. Much could be said of Master Suresh, and not all to his credit; but he wasn't stingy. Bag empty, all the brothers' hands full, the caravanmaster headed off for the Station.

"Y'all do what you want," said Mosteyfa called Teef. "But this nigga *here*?" They called him that for the obvious reason: long, snaggled, missing... "Is going all the *way* to Olorum."... pewter-black, moss-green, yellow... "My ass ain't *tryna* go right back up to the desert."... cracked, carious, crooked. "A nigga need some rest behind *that* motherfucker!"

Demane felt much the same, crudity notwithstanding. A unanimous rumble rolled across the gathering of brothers.

"Anyone?" said the captain. His right hand pantomimed a man walking away, left hand waving goodbye.

"Come this far," said some brother, "might as well go on."

"I ain't never seen Olorum, noway," said another brother.

"Silver full-boys, y'all!" said a third. "Much as we can grab, y'all!"

Captain cupped one eloquent hand behind an ear, his other urging brothers to speak up now. There could be no change of mind later.

Nobody said anything.

So the captain pointed off the route to the Station—to a field of cropped stubble and petrified goat dung. "Drills," he said. "Throwing."

The brothers groaned. They complained. The two words sufficed, however, for them to drop their packs and scramble to join Captain—already run out ahead of them onto the field and waiting. The brothers shaped up like ducklings, all in a row with their spears.

Demane tossed a couple packs off the trail to the Station, over with the other baggage. Lately wounded, Faedou eased himself down, gripping his spear like a cane.

He leaned back against the piled packs, good leg bent, trick leg outstretched. Around the back of his head some gray naps grew still, his bald pate shining like volcanic glass.

Looming against the light, Demane stayed afoot as though to see drills better. His broad stature cast commensurate shade down over his brother, seated. Sweating too much, breathing too loud, Faedou kept his face hardened against pain. The odor of infected humors coming off that bad leg stank such that Demane's sensitive tongue could *taste* the bacterial action in stagnant blood.

"You oughta let me take a quick look-see," Demane said, not for the first time. "I won't even touch my bag unless you say so. Promise."

"I told you, Sorcerer." Faedou threw an edgy glance up at Demane's bag. "I put my hopes in God."

After that last clash with bandits, Demane had tended the injuries of all the brothers save for Faedou, who, it seemed, feared the pollution of heathen arts even more than death by gangrene.

[Saprogenic possession], [antibiotic exorcism], the perils of [sepsis and necrotizing tissues] . . . Demane had perhaps doomed Faedou, in speaking such terms without knowing them in a common language. To superstitious ears, nothing distinguished those untranslated words from the veriest babble of demon worship. "If that leg get *too* bad, old man, the only thing will save you is chopping it off."

Faedou rocked side to side. "Prayer and trust in Him. His justice and mercy: that's all I need. Maybe I'll wade in the Blood of the River soon. That's all right. I asked the Dove to come down to my shoulder long ago. Won't you ask Him too, brother? For it's said in the Recital of Life and Days—"

"Yeah, yeah, yeah!"

You had to catch them quick—these more religious northerners—or they'd go on that way for a *while*. Why not get the old man talking about something useful? Nobody except the captain had crisscrossed this quarter of the continent more than Faedou. And so Demane asked about the Wildeeps.

"A strange place, nowhere else like it. Rains a lot down there, but you get sick of it after the first couple days . . ."

Demane listened, keeping an eye on drills. No matter how often he'd seen the captain's reckless feats of speed and skill, every time was still astonishing. Captain ran far out or in close, depending on the strength of a given brother's throwing arm. One at a time, they cast spears at him, aimed to kill. He either batted the spear aside or snatched it from the air, and dropped it to the dust. "Foul," he called or, if some rare effort merited encouragement, "Not bad." A brother ran to fetch his spear only after Captain had passed three men farther down the line.

"Wildeeps must be far away," Demane said. "Ain't much rain falling around these parts."

"Naw, they real close by." Faedou waved southward. "It won't take half a day to get there. See the Daughter?" Faedou pointed to the river that wound southwest, out-flowing from Mother of Waters. "A few leagues south of here, Daughter runs into another river called the Crossings that goes straight west. Other side of the Crossings, it's the Wildeeps. You'll see what I mean soon enough. It don't make no kind of sense. North of the Crossings, the land's just like this: dried up, nothing much growing. On the south, it's all green. Thick brush, and elephant grass. Jungle. The Road pick up there, south of the Crossings." Faedou faced away and spat. "That's some more ole witchcraft."

"Captain said the Wildeeps dangerous." *Do me a favor, D., will you? Get around to all the brothers and warn them not to stray off-Road when we come to the Wildeeps. Make every brother understand his life depends on obeying. It does. In the Wildeeps there is no safety, except on the Road.*

"Well, there's beast and thing, Sorcerer. *Terrible things*—what God Hisself couldn't love. Last time I went through, I swear I seen . . ."

"What, Faedou? What you see?"

" . . . I don't know, man. Maybe I *didn't* see nothing."

"Aw, come on—what, Faedou? Don't be like that!"

In motion the captain had the look of a cheetah. Long-legged, swift, too thin. He whirled left and right, away from cast spears, catching some as they passed. At the last man in line, he began back the other way. Ten or so of these circuits was the usual length of drills. After long weeks of Captain's training, the brothers had the rhythm down. Everyone either threw, sprinted to retrieve his spear, sprinted back to his place in line, or else was bent over, gasping for breath.

"Something like a crocodile. But up on two legs, you know? Mouth just *full* of teeth! Each one as bad as a knife, Sorcerer. If that thing had bit you, it would of took out as much as my two hands could grab." Faedou put his palms together at the wrists, curving his fingers like fangs: clamping down on his own thigh by way of demonstration.

"Mighty big bite," Demane agreed. "Anybody else see this thing, Faedou?"

All earthly creatures shared a common scent, the tellurian signature. But (to Demane's nose) a rare few smelled also of the stars, as if some subset of their ancestors sprang from other dust than this. There were mortal men and women in the captain's lines of descent, yes, but the gods abounded too. That voice of his, for one; and who but a cousin descended from the Towers could manage such fast footwork? The captain was plainly too strong, as well, for a man hardly more than cord and bone. Demane reckoned that Captain cut loose this way at drills, and in battle, for brief respite from the terrible self-restraint he imposed on all his deeds, movements, and even speech at other times.

"Just me. But I ain't crazy, Sorcerer. So don't be looking at me like that. I *seen* it. In the middle of the night, I got up to pee. And *seen* it by the moonlight: right over in some trees. Standing close as that patch of weeds you see right there."

"Well, how come you didn't just wake up some—"

"*I was scared*, is how come. You should of seen that damn thing! Tall as the captain, Sorcerer, I swear it was. Walking around like anybody. Teeth like this!"

"All right, all right. So, what it do next?"

Captain was eating sunlight. *Tasting* the sun, rather, for he couldn't absorb much through that headscarf he always wore. Darkling about the captain's head was a heliovore's nimbus, a sort of counterhalo—shadowy, half-starved and imperceptible to all eyes present, except Demane's. *I wish you'd take off that stupid scarf,* Demane thought, not for the first time. *What does it matter if they see your hair? You'd gain weight, strength, decades of life . . .*

"Nothing. Just stood watching the camp from the forest. After a while the walking-alligator went back up into the trees. But that's why everybody keep to the Road going through the Wildeeps. That bad stuff you hear about happen to caravans who go off-Road."

Demane said, "I don't see what the Road got to do with it."

"I told you. *Witchcraft.*" Faedou sprinkled that word around like a cook sprinkles salt: applicable to any and every dish, useful for all occasions. Perhaps in some sense it was "witchcraft" when Demane waved his hand through a cloud of mosquitoes, and then nobody else was bitten the rest of the night. But was it "witchcraft" when some unlucky brother stubbed his toe? Or bit down on sandy grit in his porridge? *Everything* can't be witchcraft! "It's them magi live down by Olorum who made the Road. Put some kind of hoodoo on it: to keep off beasts and thing. But *you* oughta know more about all this demon-raising business than me. Right, Sorcerer?"

Demane sighed. Back home in the green hills, they had called him *Mountain Bear* for his unusual size and strength. On this side of the continent, he'd picked up another name, no matter how many times he said, I ain't nobody's "sorcerer," just call me *Demane.* He obviously tried for circumspection with the petty miracles, the intelligence gleaned from preternatural senses, the things pulled from his bag in broad daylight . . . Still, he'd picked up a reputation.

Drills were done. Captain dismissed the brothers, keeping back the usual two. Demane tossed brothers their oiled goatskins full of water as they came straggling back.

Messed Up threw himself down in the grass and began to guzzle. Every time the caravan had stopped at wells in the desert, Messed Up had drunk to the point of sickness. And always, in the burning stretches between wells, he'd run short and had to come begging some of yours.

"Slow down," Demane said. "Not so much."

Teef said, "It's too *hot* for all this!" as he always did after drills. "Why the fuck Captain got us out here running around, throwing spears and shit, in the HOT ASS MOTHERFUCKEN HEAT?"

A couple other brothers—as *they* always did—said, "Amen. That's right. Why?" between sips of water.

Demane snatched the upturned goatskin from Messed Up's mouth. "How you gon' drink the whole thing straight down? You remember how you made yourself sick all them times. Act like you got some sense for once!"

"What do it matter, Sorcerer?" Once upon a time, Messed Up's scowl had only bespoken gormless passion.

"You see they got a whole big-ass lake *right there*!"

"You forgot last time already? Throwing up like that? Belly hurting? You done for now." Demane slung his arm, squeezed his hand. A silver rope of water, airborne, uncoiled above the pale dust, and then darkened a long line across it. He tossed the empty goatskin back.

These days when Messed Up scowled, whoever had thought themselves hideous could take great comfort, now recognizing themselves as beautiful. For ever since a bandit's machète had sheared half Messed Up's face from his skull—seventy-eight catgut stitches, to reattach cheek, lips, chin—*every* mug was a lovely mug by contrast with that warped leer, pulling against its sutures.

"Aw, see there?" Messed Up howled. "*Damn*, Sorcerer!" He tumbled over backwards, like some twenty-stone baby pounding his fists, kicking his heels, against the dirt.

T-Jawn, with no such lack of decorum, lay back on a grassy spot. "I should so like to sit out these drills as you do, M. Sorcier." And, peering through the slatted fingers of a languid hand, he asked, "What is your secret? *Do* tell." The question, the exhortation, sounded rhetorical to Demane, and he made to turn away. But, nay: earnestly meant, for T-Jawn sat up, asking, "No, *truly*, mon vieux: From whom did you learn such mastery of the spear?"

Demane shrugged. "My Aunty."

Brothers fell out rolling in the grass. They joked. They

laughed.

"Got my skills from Granny! Where you get yours at?"

"Was my wife learned me up. Old gal got a *arm* on her!"

"Where I come from, women hunt if they feel like it . . ." Then Demane made himself shut up. You get sick of saying the same thing over and over. Men on this side of the continent thought they were the best at everything. It was *stupid*! Aunty, however, needed his defense about as much as did Mt. Bittersmoke, where lightning struck in continuous cascade about a lake of brightly splashing lava. "Well, Captain don't go easy on me, either," Demane pointed out.

The second or third time Captain had called these drills, a near-metamorphosis had come over Demane unexpectedly. His senses sharpened, reflexes quickened, just before he'd thrown his spear. The point had caught in Captain's robe, nearly impaled him. Since then, Demane sat out drills. He and the captain sparred spear-to-spear at the end of exercises. Nor did Captain hold back much.

"I don't know about the rest of y'all, but it's *them* two little niggas"—Barkeem nodded toward the brothers still at drills—"I feel sorry for."

Demane, too. Every now and then, he'd ask Captain again to cut the hapless youngsters a little slack. "No," said the captain, without variation.

Xho Xho and Walead were all sharp elbows, skinny shanks, bony knees. So were several other brothers. None of those others, however, was so cursed with bungling hands and feet. Xho and Walé were made to throw their spears twice as many times as everyone else. Ungentle hands jerking the boys into correct stance, Captain would fix their grip on the spear, tension and turn of shoulders and hips, even how far up or down they held their chins. When a spearcast failed to please him, which was most of them, the boys had to run full out—that is, stagger, hunched over with side-stitches—back and forth a time or two from where the spear lay, back to where the captain waited, hardfaced as the fatherghost these northerners called God.

"Yo, my dudes," said a brother. "Heard they got hoes at the Station."

The truth of this hearsay was by another brother affirmed. "Yeah. Down in some tents out past the big market."

A latter beside the former two put forward his own intention, and inquired into other brothers'. "I'm heading down that way to see about one, damn betcha. Who else going?"

Nearly every brother was.

"'Bout you, Sorcerer?"

"I don't do that."

"Moi? I most certainly do," said T-Jawn for the general edification; and then, confidingly, to Demane: "Has no one informed you then, Sorcerer? After Mother of Waters, there shan't be any further opportunities to, ah— what *was* that marvelously apt phrase of yours, Barkeem?" T-Jawn popped his fingers encouragingly.

"Get your dick wet."

"*Voilà*—before we come to Olorum City?"

———————

In the green hills of home there was no such institution. And so when he'd first come from the remotest spur of the continent, to cities of the northern riviera, Demane had thought it to be a route by which men wishing to marry could meet a wife.

There, in old colonial Philipiya, skill won him the position of huntmaster for the city amir. Remunerative but silly work, bagging game for sport; and a lonely life as well, all day speaking languages other than his own, with no one to hold at night. Before a year was out, Demane had begun wondering why he'd ever traveled so far from Saxa, first love and then oldest friend, and especially from Atahly, the woman—on second thought—he really should have married. *You'll love me later as much as I love you now, and regret leaving.* She was right.

Whenever he admitted to loneliness, men of Philipiya would commend to him *whores*. Women of exceeding beauty, was the impression he'd gotten; and not to be approached without wealth. At last, he decided he'd better marry one and settle down.

The shawl cost half his savings. The amir himself had recommended the merchant. *You would need six months' travel by ship to find another like this in the world!* The silk was orange and crimson as low clouds above a sunset, stitched in thread-of-gold. Demane bought smaller treats, too, of course: pretty little bangles, candied fruit, perfume. He, the lady, and her advocates would feast together, wouldn't they? He could discreetly leave the shawl afterwards, if the lady found him congenial. The elders might like an amphora of that grape vinegar, also from overseas and costly, so beloved by Philipiya's rich . . .

The place was filthy. A long and dark hall; over doorways on the right-side wall, raggedy carpets hung. Hoarse noise and women's sobs. The fishy reek of sex unwashed for days. Reeling and flinching, his thoughts couldn't make sense of abomination. A carpet drew back on a girl much too young, lying atop stained sheets. No supper was laid out and there'd be no polite talk. He and his wife-to-be wouldn't, late in the meal, stare brazenly at each other, and then cast down their eyes again, chastened by a grunt from the chaperones. Nothing he'd imagined. Motes seethed on the verminous pallet. Who fed this little girl? Not enough. "Pretty, ain't she?" said the . . . merchant . . . proprietor? (The *pimp*, which word he hadn't known then.) "Youngest one I got. Silver penny if you want her."

Gripping the rich fringe, Demane let the shawl unfurl to the floor. He shook the bright silk aloft and let it go, draping the naked child. And left. Not so long as he lived would he forget her eyes, the misuse in them, and expectation of more.

———

"I *said*," Demane repeated, "I don't do that." His mortal mask slipped a bit askew, and he couldn't hide, for a moment, the piece of him that was perilous, a god.

T-Jawn's smirk faltered. Talk of whores diverted elsewhere, now in hushed tones, brothers leaning together like boys trading nasty whispers within earshot of the father.

Demane looked south. Coming up the path their caravan would travel down tomorrow, a northbound caravan was just arriving at the Station of Mother of Waters. Half the size of theirs, this caravan had a couple hundred burros, some fifty men, merchants and brothers. At the back of the caravan, some few dozen buffalo were driven along by men riding camels of a sort Demane had not seen before, sleek and agile.

"Buffalo riders," said Faedou, eyes too on this arrival. He like Demane cared nothing for what went on in the tents beyond the market, caring only for his two beloved wives and eleven children.

Buffalo riders? Were they? *Yes!* Look at the beaded leathers, the long locked hair, their complexion not some singular color like other peoples, but three shades at once. How did it go? *Oxblood, amber, good earth . . .* Everything just as in the tall tales and melancholy songs brothers told or sang at nightly camps. One thing puzzled Demane, though. "Ain't they suppose to *ride* the buffalo?" He'd dearly wanted to see that—some rider perched high atop a buffalo's hump and clinging, presumably, to the horns.

Faedou gave a crack of incredulous laughter. "*Ride* em?"

"Well, they called *buffalo riders*, ain't they?"

"Aw, baby . . . ! What kind of Sorcerer you suppose to be, thinking they ride buffalo, not *herd* em?"

"Leastways I don't wrestle bare-handed with bandits trying to stab me with a knife."

"Ooooooh!" said the brothers. Demane and Faedou

went back and forth for a few good-natured rounds of insult.

Xho Xho and Walead ran up. "Captain said." They blew, they puffed. "The captain said, tell that damn Sorcerer to bring his lazy, loafing ass on."

No doubt that had been the *sense* of his message. But Captain stooped neither to low speech, nor ever to profanity.

Demane rose with his spear, and punched at half-speed for Walead's head. Laughing, the boy just managed to duck away.

"Hold this." Demane tossed his bag to Cumalo. Some brothers risked a look askance; others gawped in awe at the bag. One or two made a sign against the Beast. Unlike his brothers, easygoing Cumalo suffered no pangs of either fear or curiosity. Certainly one ancient little heirloom, passed down to mortal offspring from the gods gone back to heaven, was not enough to rouse him. Bag on his chest, Cumalo resumed drowsing in the grass.

To the east, as far as sight went, there was a view of overgrazed scrub and cracked earth, all in shades of gray and dun. The weedy field of goat chips inclined slightly, the black-robed figure standing tall against morning's blue-gold sky. Captain exuded his familiar tang-spice of impatience. Demane hustled up the dry acres to him. One of them bristled and frowned, the other going downcast and quiet, whenever the two came near each other, and why? *Hatred*, said most brothers: hot and personal. No, it was *rivalry*, said others: respectful but fierce. And then some brother would mutter half of the proverb, "Two top dogs, just one pack..." and everyone would shake his head, eyes peeled for the brewing showdown.

The captain had a tic, at this very moment indulging it. His thumb and forefinger pinched along the edges of his headscarf, though the cloth was cinched too viciously tight for adjustment. As always, it covered Captain's head even down over the brows (shaved off, anyway). And snug as that scarf was tied, it was no wonder he went around squinting, mouth set in a hard line, as if his head never stopped aching. The captain had rebuffed all of Demane's inquiries into the need for disguise, and so now he gathered clues only as they dropped. It seemed Captain was nobody awash in glory or scandal, so long as that scarf stayed on. Should the wrong eyes see him with it *off*, however . . .

"Cain't see nothing," Demane said. "You got that scarf on proper, like always."

Had a scorpion bit it, that hand couldn't have quit its fussing any quicker. The captain bristled and frowned.

"First touch?" Demane handed over his spear. Captain nodded while swaddling the point of Demane's spear in thick cloth; he handed it back. His own spear-blade unscrewed from an iron mount on the shaft, already disarmed.

Signaling for the watchers' sake, Captain held up two fingers, then raised a third. Softly he sang: "Two of three."

That voice! Captain lacked the power of speech, was capable only of song. He could stand dumb, gesturing, or else make incomparable music. Even in a monosyllable, it was possible to hear him struggling to tarnish his pure tones, hoarsen their rich clarity; trying to turn his *vox seraphica* into a thing befitting the vulgar, violent world of a caravan guardsman. But calliphony was as inseparable from the captain's voice as blood from a living heart, and he could do nothing, try as he might, to make any utterance of his less than the loveliest you'd heard, or would ever hear, so long as you lived.

Captain attacked. It would seem safer to hang back from the point of another warrior's spear, and in particular that spearpoint which tracked so closely, punished so fiercely, every instant of proximity, addering in and out with venomous speed, one bite sufficient to kill. Men— nearly every man—had to work up the nerve to skip in close, thrust once and fast, and then skip backwards again, not caring so much whether they'd gotten the kill, just glad to be alive. Demane fought that way, certainly. The captain, however, lunged in close enough to deal death easily, or catch his own, and never quit such close-

31

ness until someone fell dead, never yet him.

The captain's single spear seemed two, even at times three. It darted from the billowing folds of his dark robe with murderous speed and accuracy. Demane scrambled from the thrusts, blocked the slashes. Scarcely could he steal a moment to gasp for breath between attacks. At this pace, defense was the best he could do, offense out of the question.

Then—lightly as a brush of lips—the blunt mount of Captain's spear tapped the base of Demane's throat.

Absurd control! Captain could have won the bout at any moment from the first. His own breath bellowing in his ears, Demane could hardly make out the brothers' raucous encouragement.

"Where's your fire today, Sorcerer?" So exquisite was the manner of Captain's speech, *meaning* of his words was easily missed. "Keep that spear up, and centered here or here." He tapped his chest, his belly. "And you can hardly win, can you, if you just block and flee?" To hear was like to see a majestic view of mountains; or for the first time, some city teeming with its thousands—such a chill and creep of gooseflesh as that, such wonder . . . "So *attack* me, man. Attack!"

Next bout. Demane bullied in closer as Captain had often advised him to do, and there his greater strength and heavier spear seemed to tell. Either Demane fought better, or the captain began to tire at last from his mad exertions. They made the same attack, spears harpooning in. Demane parried. The captain spun aside, but coming too near. Without thinking, Demane threw a punch of the sort that cracks a skull, snaps the neck. But didn't connect—for Captain leaned back easily from that fist, his face just beyond the knuckles. Even so, the spontaneous strike earned Demane a rare "Good!" and a glissando of surprised laughter, Captain's body releasing the thrill-scent of a fearless man just brushing death.

Right at that moment, the swaddling cloth slipped from Demane's spearpoint.

There was no moment to disarm the spear again, for Captain, careless that he faced a live spearpoint, jabbed his own shaft with killing force, pressing the offense. Caring in the captain's stead, Demane gave way and offered only defense. Long practice, however—and Captain's own masterful training—had ingrained new reflexes in Demane. Those quick feet—always so sure—chanced to stumble, and caution could not quite check the instantaneous drive of Demane's spear.

The captain should have, as always before, made a light-footed sideways spin. But, as never before, Captain faltered a second time, flat-footed in just the right position to die.

Two things occurred: one thought, one action.

Demane pulled the strike, of course—hauling back and jerking it aside with violence sufficient to knock himself over. Even so, the blade pierced the captain's robe and some flesh too. And Demane's thought?

He did that on purpose.

Captain tossed his head, meaning *Get up*. Demane didn't rise, staying sprawled on the ground. There was never any time or space for open talk between them, so they'd learned to say a great deal with expression alone. Demane would not play, not with these rules; he made that clear to Captain. Whose face hardened, whose blunted spear darted forwards, a blow that would not feel nice. For the captain held firmly that any insubordination from a man under his command was best answered with the hardest of knocks. Bandits and corsairs, intent upon murder, hadn't hit Demane so hard as this man.

Would Captain knock the wind from him? A gut-blow? Or would the steel base crack against his forehead, raising an egg? A strike to the mouth, bursting a lip, chipping some tooth . . . ? The plunging spear halted a hair's breadth above Demane's navel—content, today, to mime the blow and deal none. *Captain wins!*

Demane knocked the shaft aside. "Isa! Did I hurt you?" He got up. "*Why* did you—?"

"Call me Captain." He wound a fist in his loose robe, pressing the wadded cloth to his side. "Don't get your people mixed up, brother." Sun in his eyes, the captain had pretext by which to turn about, his back now to the brothers' shouts: facing Demane and winning them a moment's semiprivacy. The aspect of cruel command left the captain's face, abruptly as if he'd removed a mask. No one had ever looked so changed! There was a deep story here, some great wrong done: how had this man meant only for the gentle and the good been conscripted into service of violence and pain?

You cannot fix the whole world's pain, Demane; there's too much. But what about one man's, Aunty? Can I do that much?

"Listen, D.," Captain sang not in his customary register, *stonehills,** but in the one Demane liked, far lovelier. "Would you help me with something?"

"*Yeah,* but why—and let me see—"

"Stop, man." Captain brushed the hand away. "It's just a scratch. Listen to me." He said such things as—*See to the others, I wasn't hurt; it's nothing; I'm fine; I don't feel it*—turning aside all help, although he knew, for Demane had warned him the first day they'd met, that all lies were

---

* Baritone *con squillo.* A voice to be heard, in every sense: clarion-like over the din of skirmish, agonies, and war-cries; and as daunting to his own as to the enemy.

barefaced to Demane's hypersenses. Scent testifies against a liar, and subtle flinches; a stuttering pulse and mistimed blinks, the tremors and halts of the voice: there were a *thousand* tells . . . Demane couldn't help but know truth from falsehood.

The captain faced about again, so all could see him. No longer fey, his face resumed a falcon's arrogance. "Tell the brothers they'd best behave in the Station. At Mother of Waters, the fort soldiers don't play. If the fo-so are called out because some brother is wilding, the caravan-master pays a fine in silver full-weight. You know what Suresh will say then. *Leave that fool here at the edge of the desert, with nothing,* or maybe he'll say, *Let the brother come with us, but I'll take it from his pay.* Either way, it's a bad outcome for that brother."

Demane nodded. He watched to see whether a be-soaking gleam would come through the cloth Captain held bunched to his side. *Nothing* would put him off if that robe showed wet.

"Oh," said the captain, "and if *I'm* the one who catches some brother raising a ruckus . . ."

Where had that glimpse of surpassing peace gone? Now there was nothing to be seen in the captain but what long and bloody allegiance to war had made of him. If just he'd *talk* to the others, too, and let them come to *know* him truly; *joke* with the brothers sometimes, sit *beside* them in easy fraternity. Then there'd be no need to threaten a savage beatdown to get them jumping to obey him . . . ! Demane gave as much of this advice as he could: "All right, Captain; I'll tell em. But—"

"Not the time or place. Are you going to set me on fire right here, D.? In front of everybody?"

Demane shook his head.

Hand pressed to his side, Captain jogged up to the Station.

———————

"You almost *got* him! That was *gold*, my nigga. Not fake, not fool's, not dross: GOLD. Nigga, it was some *official* shit you just did, almost beating the captain like that! That, my nigga, was straight up gold-plated LIKE SHIT."

Demane wrapt a prodigious hand about Walead's nape. With the greatest gentleness, he gave the boy to know how wringably his narrow neck secured his small skull. "How many times I told you, Walé? I don't *like* that word."

"I know, Sorcerer—sorry! Captain just mad, though, cause you almost beat him!"

"For real, Sorcerer; you came *this* close. You got just about his same speed, and *more* stremf!"

"Don't let the man worry to you, son. He just evil like

37

that. *Always* in a bad mood."

Their shadows still west-leaning and longish in the forenoon, Demane and his brothers walked up toward the Station. They always surprised him. To Demane, the captain's front was flimsy and collapsed with the slightest scrutiny. But the brothers stayed convinced, believing Captain to be precisely what he seemed. Demane told them as much of the truth as he could: "Listen up. Y'all know we cain't carry these spears around the Station, right . . . ?"

But none of us would step forward, and we did beg *her* to be master. She though refused us, saying, Ever since the isle broke and the Towers returned to heaven, I have remained here planetbound, protector of all earthly beings. Now I wish to see the galaxies. Are you all so troubled then, that one of you little powers should become very great?

We answered that it terrified us, one and all, to be bound forever to that wild tract of land, with nowhere to go, nothing to do . . .

Our ignorance amazed her, and she laughed at our fears, saying, How can it be, still, that you understand so little? *Whosoever take charge of the Wild Depths shall have the freedom of any place and time among all the worlds that touch and overlap there. They may come and go between universes,* do you understand? And when it should come to pall, such long life, such mastery of time and space, only let the master pass custodianship to another, some youthful power of good heart: and then

rise up as light to join the gods beyond the sky, even as
I am about to do . . .

from [ancestral eidetic memory] of the magi
of the Ashëan Enclave

Second of Seven

Only mud came up from the wells at Ajeric, no water. That sometimes happened, and most of the caravan had rationed for it; but many hadn't. One among the guardsmen, Gangy, who'd been spendthrift with his water, began to mutter in a manner damaging to brotherly morale. It would begin by feeling your eyes dry tearless and unblinkable, said Gangy, your tongue swelling blueblack in your mouth, and skin shriveling up into leather, into jerky. Perhaps a year hence, some wayfarer would spot a skull scoured meatless by the sands, sun-bleached: *yours*—The seditious remainder cut short by the hard back of Captain's hand. They would all reach the next wells alive, said Master Suresh, so long as grown men didn't sit and weep, boo hoo hoo like some sad whore, her six best boys lost this week to marriage. We must do now as she did then: dry the tears, and *hustle!*

The caravan pressed on. There was no talk, no sound, except the jingling of harness and the vague shush of sands shifted by their passage.

Every night the brazen sphere dissolves in a molten

line, compelling the gaze westward when the sky's dark otherwise. With a similar compulsion, the least dampness in the driest wastes would seize Demane's whole attention. No stopping at nightfall, nor for midnight, either: the caravan was still going after moonset. Under cloudless constellations, the camels trudged along the banks of a dead river, extinct since prehistory. They came to a stretch of arroyo where humidity hovered, where some deep spring leaked up even to the surface. Demane snapped the reins of his camel, hurrying the beast from midpack to the caravan's forefront, where Captain rode.

Master Suresh kept watch on all such urgencies. He too brought his camel up abreast, in time to see Demane's gesture and hear the offending word. "Water?" the caravanmaster cried. "Succubee of thirst and mirage! They have fucked out that man's brains, Captain. Tell your fevered brother: this river died before the dragons burnt Daluça!"

The captain ran every day, and much farther on some, whether for penance or harder exercise, who knew. That day he'd run from Ajeric's wells until after sundown. He'd only just mounted his camel. With heart-spoke fatigue, he looked at Demane. *Are you sure? Don't make a fool of me.*

"I'm telling you, Captain." Demane pointed again down the arroyo's draw. "It's good water right there."

Captain turned to the caravanmaster and gave beautiful corroboration. "It's yours to say: stop or go on. But the water *is* here, Master Suresh." The master muttered vile curses—not really doubting, though. The captain's word had weight.

"Hold here!" the master bellowed to his caravan.

Spades, mallet, chisel. Demane chose Messed Up, Michelo, Wock, and the captain himself: the men strongest in the caravan. The long draw was more rock than sand, but not steep. By dim stars, the chosen picked their way down. The silver night ablaze for him, Demane ran ahead to where wetness rose richest, near a boulder.

Bent over, noses in the sand and pressed to the rim of the half-ton slab, even the others could smell it. But there was no trickle, only a dark stain in the sand. Nor could they shift the stone, and to bring down more hands would only crowd and hinder, not help.

"Let me try something," Demane said. He had the captain give his highest, sharpest cries, and listening to echoes the rock returned, chose a spot to crouch. He milked his third eye for vitriol. It took time, and to the others it seemed that Demane only knelt, lost in thought or prayer for water. He'd once accomplished this feat as a boy, when still a novice, but never since in earnest.

Master Suresh called down bitterly.

Dolce, the captain called back.

Some time later, Messed Up nudged Demane's shoulder. "Damn, Sorcerer." He breathed by mouth, and poked Demane again. "Why you just *setting there*?" Demane tried to wave him off, focusing on the contract-release of the tiniest, most obscure muscles.

Captain pulled Messed Up back.

Mouth full, Demane bowed and pressed his lips to a crack under the rock. He spat hard. Weak phosphoros was hid by his body, but the rock cried out—inorganic cavils and groans. "*¡Coño!*" "The fuck was *that*?" the brothers exclaimed. Virulent potency sheared deep feet through rock, and then sinking, smelted and cracked the stone. Igneous fumes, *hot*, hissed out. Demane jumped up and back with the rest. When the fiery stink had cleared, Captain waved Demane beside him, and the other three to the rock's opposite side. This time their strength sufficed to tip the boulder out from the greater shelf beneath. They sent it on its way, sliding to the sandy bottom.

"Pero no veo naá . . ." Wock began, and then *heard*. So did they all: a burbling sigh, the sweet sound of water pissing through fractured stone; then saw the starlit froth too, as it welled up, running away in glitters over the thirsty sand and gravel. Messed Up fell greedily to hands and knees.

"*Water*," Captain sang to the ridge above. "*Come*

down." The caravan came.

———————

Abundant water flowed with the effect of wine. The caravan drank and drank and lay down anywhere. Brothers should have known the routine. Five different men guarded each quarter of the night, while four slept the night through. They'd done so more than eighty times already, at every sleep-camp when Captain called the watch. But by the lucky springs, so late it would dawn soon, Captain sat for a moment in the sand. And it must surely have felt soft to him, for he began to nod, his lips slackening. Across camp, watching between slow blinks, Demane lay stretched out already. It had been a long day of highs and lows; he too was at lowest ebb. His knack for medicinals, as it turned out, had proved no help at all with venoms. That feat had drained Demane to the dregs. He ought to practice more, but why, *nasty* stuff . . . Demane slept too.

Some nightmare woke him. The fleshcolored sky was sallowing in the orient. Over the lip of the ridge, down the arroyo's east bank, ragged shapes with machètes or spears loped from rock to rock, sliding where their footing crumbled, descending on the caravan asleep in the bottom sands. Thirty? No, there were *fifty* of them at least!

Desperados.

Demane's alarums woke the camp. Snoring brothers took hard kicks. Some sleepers he snatched up by the hair and dropped on foot awake. As soon as Demane began to yell, every bandit set up whooping, lunatic as hyenas. Twice the number of blades bristled downslope as up, and there was nobody silent, everyone screaming. Before the teeth of spears could chew them, the merchants scrambled past the brothers to cower against the western bank; and then top and bottom jaw of the skirmish closed. The merchants all lived. Brothers died.

Where was Captain? Amidst the enemy already, a blur of black robes, quarter-way-up the eastern slope in the thick of them. The captain went from one to another, inspiring shrill agony or utter silence as he passed. By sixes and sevens the bandits would close with him before he got the numbers down. A full half dozen pressing together could scrawl shallow wounds on him, or rend his robe. Captain in turn pocked the crush with every movement.

Chickenty thought he was a hero too. Though Demane called him back where the brothers rallied at the bottom, Chickenty ran on upslope. He speared one desperado, and then another behind that first. He engaged a third. Weeks before, in the last raid, he'd worked wonders with his quick feet on firm ground. But sand shifts and rolls, worse on the uphill, and no one's feet can be as fast or sure. Some fourth desperado came driving in on Chick's blindside, and he *did* hear Demane's warning shout. But his step sideways was not quick enough, and he slipped. The spear skewered Chick kidney-to-kidney. Crumpling sidewise, he vomited blood, and was the first brother to die.

There is a principle called TSIM. Through deep time the universe complicates, all things whatsoever arising from the mother quantum, precisely so this man (writhing now on Demane's spearpoint) might enjoy sentience, choice, and love. This is TSIM. And all who claim to follow the principle must have hands loath and cold when it comes time to kill. You're sworn to better work than murder. Unreckoned aeons gone by, and incalculable effort spent, for what? To kill a man, your unctuous shaft dragging, slippery and bone-caught, through your grasp? Demane braced his foot to the deadman's chest, crushing ribs and sternum under his heel, until his spearpoint pulled loose. Clear as day he heard the Tower laughing on its left side: TSOA. Chaos and pointlessness *are* the point! That is TSOA. But divinity knocked about inside Demane like some great-winged bird caught indoors, frantic to find that one open window again; and so, however slow and reluctant, still he had faster hands, stronger arms, than anyone facing him.

Xho Xho, Walead, and Bou, clumsy runts all three, wisely kept together. Four times they repeated the same maneuver—scatter, flank, triple-thrust—that Captain had taught them. But then Walead came up tardy on the left and Bou, in front, died for it. So too might have Xho Xho, when the bandit whirled right, wolf-howling. Demane threw his spear into the man's warcry. Bad teeth had clamped onto the shaft when Demane wrenched his spearhead out.

Messed Up roared and stabbed. A wattle of gore, long and red, dangled off his jaw. The seemly flesh had been laid back, his bloodwashed molars in naked discovery, also the bones of his cheek and jaw, and much busy undergristle besides. Desperados scattered away from him. But Messed Up caught them, and killed them, anyway. Rats in rout, with the ratter giving chase! Behold the wake of strewn bodies, and here comes the big one himself, redtoothed and crazed. About the business best suiting him.

No one could save Wock. Nor the twins, Cruz and Glório. Demane didn't even know they'd died 'til afterwards.

Teef and Barkeem, hemmed in by mayhem. Hard pressed by two bandits, T-Jawn scrabbled for footing on a steep patch of sand. He fell, slaughter-ready, before both spears. Demane was too far away to rescue any of the three. Not the captain, though; he swooped in, with the same acts dealing death and deliverance. The point and edge of his spear opened red lips in one bandit's throat. Lifesblood emptied from that new mouth, while the other bandit took the same blow's downstroke, which cored his heart. Captain made the body dance with the twist-jerk of freeing his spear. Beside the two abruptly dead, one of the desperadoes attacking Teef quailed and ran. Captain threw his spear half through the fleeing man's back. He left the corpse transfixed, and yanked his old-style Daluçan knife from its baldric. Called, properly, "sword," the blade was arm's length, and much too long to ply for eating, hunting, or any use apart from war. Barkeem backed from some long-armed bandit who had two daggers, twin snakes, striking from either hand. Captain, in the act of drawing his sword, took the top off that bandit's head. Crown and brow slid, widthwise, from cheeks and jowls. Walead and Xho Xho were in straits again. The captain flew to their salvation—not as some crow might, but his robes as black as wings, and covering the ground as swiftly.

Demane killed the man he fought, and the hot excess of bandit's blood provoked a vision, a moment of retrospect, or of some life unlived. Bangles, khol'd eyes, ankles chiming tiny bells. The captain's naked torso, lithe and rippling. His thighs half-clad in gauze of gold, loins in leopard suede. Some history that might have been, or had been: the captain dancing for the Olorumi sovereign or Kidanese empress. When that august hand waved to clear a marble hall, one hot glance said to him: *You, stay.* Demane glimpsed shadows of a world forgone in Captain's prosecution of the counterattack. Had nimble limbs turned to other purposes, had they cultivated a different grace. Demane saw some brother down.

Faedou rolled apart from a throttled corpse, the dead man still clutching a knife driven into living flesh. Faedou pried off the futile grip, and plucked the blade from his thigh. On first and second attempt, he couldn't stand. By the third, Demane had reached him and was kneeling. "Sorcerer . . . , " Faedou panted shallowly, " . . . *head up!*"

Some mother's son tilted downhill. About thirteen years old, maybe *twelve*, the bandit boy held his spear as mounted men hold a lance. There was time and space enough for Demane to throw his spear, but he didn't. Even a moment later, his reach being much longer, Demane might have simply angled up his spear. Running headlong, the boy would have impaled himself on the point, like a chunk of meat on a skewer. Instead, Demane dropped his spear and caught the boy's with one hand, just below the point.

Though slowed, the boy wasn't stopped. Faedou howled and curled like a beetle, his leg kicked or trod in the scuffle. Demane's palm burned as the spearshaft greased down his bloodslick grip. The leverage was all wrong for him, perfect for the boy: on the downhill, speeding weight behind him, a two-handed grip. Demane had thrown his right and stronger hand back, braced to the ground, to keep himself from reeling ass over end. The child bore down, driving with desperate strength. Chapped lips snarling back from whitest teeth.

This was not the way he'd thought he'd die. But as the spearpoint broke skin on his chest, Demane felt only sublime relief: TSIM. No one else's son would die by his hands today, or ever again. Then *red gleamed,* sunlight on wet steel. Smitten off, the boy's head flew, fell, rolled away downhill. Arterial jets from the stump spewed brighter amidst darker dribble. It listed, its knees buckled, and rather than drop the corpse went subsiding down in stages, to bow over and decant headless onto the sands. Captain—

———

"No, *wait!*"

Xho Xho grabbed Demane's arm, swinging off his feet for a moment like a little monkey on a big branch. "We cain't go in Mother of Waters like this. We gotta go in through *there.*" Through the great gates puncturing the squat tower on the east, the boy meant, pointing a finger thither. Thick as a man was tall, and painted over with bright murals, adobe ramparts walled only the eastern boundary of the Station. Demane would have led them into town up a shepherds' path, on the south side.

"Yeah, I know it's strange, Sorcerer," the boy said. "I can see what you mean about the walls. But the fo-so don't play." Xho Xho had been born at Mother of Waters—or in a tent outside the Station, anyway. "It's the *rules*: caravans come in through the gates."

Foreign taboos, Demane decided.

He sent them on ahead, where fort soldiers were collecting spears beneath the tower. Waving Cumalo to follow, he crouched outside, beside the painted walls. "Stand there, will you?" Demane pointed him into place. The two of them hailed from the same remote spur of the continent, and in these parts that made them countrymen. After the native fashion, Cumalo dressed in a voluminous black robe: perfectly suited to blocking the view of passersby.

Demane opened his bag. He stuck his seven-foot spear down into it.

"Hey, as long as you've got that bad boy open . . . ," Cumalo said. "Do you care if I hold a couple pennies for you, at least 'til we get to Olorum?"

Demane dug out a careless pinch of savings. He stood and handed the coins over uncounted.

"Aw, Sorcerer. This is too much! All I need is—"

"Don't worry about it. Come on." Demane laid a hand on Cumalo's back, guiding him back toward the gates. There was a hard talk about gambling in the offing. Cumalo had never made bride-price, and so his lady up north in Philipiya still lived with her parents: two big boys, one baby girl, and twelve long years into an uneasy approximation of marriage. An ugly possibility troubled Demane's mind. Could a good friend, your homeboy, also be a shiftless, trifling ne'er-do-well?* He looked up at the painted wall.

A hero and his second, beset on all sides by a multinational host, were putting down the enemy with extreme prejudice. No man Demane had met was his match for strength, but the one painted centermost might surpass him in girth and brawn, if true to life. The hero's right

---

* This hard talk with Cumalo kept getting postponed too because—let's be honest here—the economics of civilization baffled Demane; no, really, they bored him stupid: bride-price, gambling, the wherefore a half-weight of gold gets you *this* many silver pennies, while some entirely different exchange the other way around. Aunty used to say that whatever you skip learning is the one thing you'll end up needing to know most later. But the money-game was unbelievably fussy and rulebound: which little metal counter, and how many of them, and when, and why, for this, for that, for the other thing . . . One of these days Demane meant to get to grips with it all. Real soon now. Yeah.

arm bulked with muscle still within human bounds. But that left arm was superhuman, and would have massed as thick as Demane's thigh. It was the left hand, too, that gripped a rock-hewn axe depicted midstroke, dashing open fully half the front rank of foemen's skulls. Five heads were as many eggs of bone, blood, brains bursting behind the sweep of the spiked stone that crowned the hero's weapon. Five more crouched in a desperate scrum, transfixed before the fall of the meteor toward *their* heads. Beside the hero, his second lay about him with a Daluçan knife—a "sword"—scything the close-ranked enemy as might a farmer his corn. Scattered fingers, another hand still on its forearm, a head cloven crosswise, the crown of another with the cranial bowl dumping its jellies: these and other fruits of the flesh tumbled pell-mell in a grisly harvest. Neither the expression nor appearance of the hero's second was marked out in particular detail, save for the coloring of his warrior braids. Those paints glistened as bright as agate or lapis lazuli.

"It's showing the battle of Sweet Wells Station," Cumalo said.

Demane asked, "Who's he?"

"Big one's the Lion of Olorum. Generalissimo and the prince the old King chose to rule after him. But a two-headed mamba bit him and he died. The one with the long knife is—*was*—his right hand. The Lion loved his women and left twentysome wives, twice as many children; but those two, well, they say . . ." Cumalo looked at Demane askance, and, thinking again, said only, "That blue hair is really something, huh?"

Demane shrugged.

Through the gates was a view down the Mainway, to the bustle on the piazza at the Station's center and farther, to the glimmer of Mother of Waters. Folk and beasts glutted the Mainway's length with all the noise and stench to be expected in-town.

Under-tower, a dozen fort soldiers mingled with the brothers. The fo-so handed out reclamation chits, collecting spears. They wore black robes, strung-bead commemorials of past actions; the youngbloods' hair was plaited in looping designs, the oldheads in simple cornrows. The fo-so were all unmixed Olorumi, and therefore beardless as babies; their right cheeks smooth, the others finely mutilated. Insignia of a thornwasp, the one-stinger drone, was cut into every left cheek.

" . . . vouchsafed none but them keeping to the Road. Certain doom befalls . . ."

"This for *that*? Unt uh! This spear was my . . ."

"Naw, you niggas right on time, matterfact. They got *all* the fights going today. Dogs, birds, dudes . . ."

A wealthy merchant, in robes dyed the deepest color of lilies, remonstrated with the garrison's commandant, whose cicatrix boasted three stingers, a thornwasp prince-of-nest. A handful of fo-so wore breastplates weathered by rust or verdigris; the commandant's, however, was made of some mirror-polished alloy, flashing even in the shadows under-tower. Not quite able to make out the discussion between the merchant and elite soldier in so much crosstalk and din, Demane sidled closer.

The merchant had just come in with that smaller caravan, fresh off the route Master Suresh l'Merqerim meant to follow tomorrow. Standing attendance on the merchant was a man prepossessing as only brothers were: thick-thewed, with a brawler's ears, nose, and scars. His master was most insistent: "And yet, that is precisely what we *did* do. Do you think us fools? All the way through the Wildeeps, not a man jack set foot off the safe way!"

"Then we have misspoken," said the fo-so in the gorgeous cuirass, "and do most humbly beg your pardon." A man hopes, of course, to inoculate others with his own sense of serenity, by employing that tranquil tone and placid pose. A shame, then, it serves only to infuriate! "Yet we must request that you please moderate your—"

"You fail to *listen*. What I am trying to *tell* you, if you could *hear* it, is that some eater of men—a lion, *some*thing—hunted us south to north across the Wildeeps. Seven men, *seven* (can you see these fingers?

well, count them, then: *seven*!) were dragged away in the night. Eaten alive, screaming! The beast came onto the Road. I shall repeat that, for the salient detail here seems not to penetrate your stopped-up ears. *Onto* the Road, man!" As the merchant became exercised, his guardsman shifted impatiently in place. The brother's coloring was the ruddy-dark iridescence of a plainsman buffalo rider. When he moved, and bone or brawn pressed from beneath the skin, his complexion paled or darkened, going redbone, redbrown, dark brown across his face and bare arms. "There was a caravan some days behind us. Others from the Station will be going south. What of them? You must send down a party of soldiers and root the thing out!"

"Would that our remit did extend to such adventures." The commandant spoke in round tones, with graceful gestures. "But here at Mother of Water's garrison, our warrant is the security and defense of this Station, not the mounting of bold expeditions into the bush. Therefore, lacking leave from His Holiest Majesty in Olorum, we must regrettably . . ."

Messed Up roared. "This was my *Daddy* spear! Fuck if I'm selling it for no chip of wood on a leather *string*! Y'ALL MUSTA LOSS Y'ALL DAMN MIND." He threw deadly elbows, shaking his shaggy head, and the brothers couldn't calm him. Somehow Messed Up had lost none of his corpulent powers to the rigors of the desert crossing. Not easily, then, did Demane bind that tantrum within an embrace.

"I got him, y'all, I got him," Demane told the others. "Go ahead into the Station. We catch up later."

He got Messed Up out past the gates into the bright sun.

Messed Up's eye on the wounded side was squinching tight-shut, and then bugging wide-open. That cheek tic'd; it juddered—not one of his good days.

"Tomorrow when we go, you just hand em that little piece of wood on the string, and you get the spear back. *Your* spear. Nobody else's. Feel me?" Demane wondered what other words might explain check and reclamation . . . but then Messed Up meekly nodded.

(And why now? Was this yet more strange sorcery? No: gratitude. After the clash with bandits outside Ajeric, hadn't the Sorcerer sewn Messed Up whole and fine again, when half his face hung off—hung down—like a flag with no wind to lift it? Hadn't the Sorcerer bathed that terrible wound, dressed it soft-handedly; slathered all manner of things over it, some cool, some that cut the nightmarish pain? Now it hardly hurt! No, the Sorcerer's assurances did not make sense, but Messed Up would offer him this leap of faith anyhow. A gift.)

They went in. Messed Up surrendered his spear.

"Bet be RIGHT HERE, too, when I come tamara!" Messed Up shouted at the soldier who stowed the spear in the armory with the rest. Xho Xho and Walead hustled their brother out.

A fo-so turned to Demane. "That's all you brought with you?" He gestured to the little bag hanging at Demane's left hip. "Where's your gear at, your weapons?"

A soldier beside the first leaned over to his friend, whispering (a baseline human could never have overheard): "Naked-ass bush savages. Shouldn't even let they ass up *in* here!"

A number of petty miracles lay within Demane's power. His reflexes, his strength, were rather better than even the most gifted of athletes'; and his sense of sight and smell, and so on, could wax exceedingly keen at times. But the blood of TSIMtsoa ran thin in him, and it seemed he could not manage the metamorphosis into great power. Even so, provoke him enough, and the provoker *would* catch a glimpse—radiant, dark—of the stormbird. Demane spread his empty hands.

"What you see," he said, "is what I got."

A peaceable gesture: and yet one fo-so ducked his head, shuffling, while the other grinned with all his teeth, and said, "'Joy your stay at Mother of Waters!"

With a bob of the chin, Demane accepted the greeting.

———————

Wilfredo wandered off into the westbound traffic on the Mainway.

Teef, Barkeem, T-Jawn, and a couple others were headed to the Fighthouse. Cumalo told them the way.

Faedou limped off north, into labyrinthine alleys.

The remaining brothers either took roost on the split-rail fence or else leaned against the posts of the garrison paddock just round back the tower. "What*ever* you looking for, y'all can find it up in the piazza," Xho Xho was telling these first-timers. At nightfall, daytime commerce cleared from the piazza "and they kimmel† a greatorch right in the middle." Hundreds would dance and dozens drum until dawn . . .

It came to Demane that someone should spare a thought for where brothers would have to meet the caravan tomorrow. Human bustle and metallic bits, however—countless and reflective—were flickering nauseously in the corners of Demane's eyes. Dense aerosols clogged his nose and tongue, smell and taste inundated with clamorous trivia. Loud, low, soft, shrill: the Station

———————

† Enkindle?

was a high tide of talk, a stormy sea of noise, wave after wave swamping him.

Xho Xho's disquisition began to cover local outlets for black market and sin. Here as elsewhere, a silver penny was the going rate; but niggas should not sleep on the fact that, up in the piazza after midnight, there would be mad hoes out, offering *deep* discounts . . . Demane lay a pastoral hand on the boy's shoulder.

"Oh, right, my man. Sorry!" Xho Xho shifted his restless gaze over the Mainway's traffic. "You *had* said you wasn't trying to get into nothing nasty." The boy, though, was, for bitter, and yet ineffably saccharine, was the aroma of mischief. And Xho Xho stank of it.

A wise man would grab hold of this boy, and get honest answers to hard questions. But Demane let the intuition go by. Squinting, his teeth achy from gritting, he hadn't yet moderated his senses for city extremes. "Just tell me, Xho," Demane said, "where at, tomorrow, we suppose to meet up with the caravan?"

Following the boy's vague gesture, Demane looked across the teeming Mainway. Master Suresh and merchants could not be seen unloading over at that first complex of stables, corrals, and warehouses. "*Where*, Xho? Someplace on the south side of the Station, you mean?"

"Yeah, Sorcerer. Over there." Xho Xho eyed and dismissed every passing face, as though in hope or dread of one he knew. "Master Suresh got one of the biggest outfits *at* Mother of Waters. Cain't miss it. Ask anybody." The boy slithered out from under the shepherding hand. "Well, let me get up with you brothers later at the piazza tonight. All right? I need to go holler real quick at these niggas I used run with. *Yo, Walé!* I'm out! You coming or what?"

"Yeah! Hold up! *Damn!*"

What if, as Walead and Messed Up took off after Xho Xho up the Mainway, Demane had only shouted, *Hey, y'all be good! Hear me?* What then?

His eyes were shut, though. He was rubbing his temples.

The brothers scattered.

Cumalo stayed. "What is it, that in-city thing bothering you? Can I help?"

" . . . No." Demane blinked and looked around, the sense-ruckus quieting into lucidity. "It's better now. I'm all right."

"Well, come on," Cumalo said. "I've got a surprise for you." He took Demane's hand and tugged.

A block down from the piazza was a shantytown of food vendors. They stopped at a dingy stall and offered she who worked there warm greetings and smiles. The old woman blinked at them, seeming put out by this interruption of her boredom. It was not at first certain that

Cumalo's courteous request and nugget of rock salt would suffice to stir the concessionaire into sullen motion. She slapped the salt onto the countertop, chose a consequent fragment, and popped it into her mouth. Twice—voluptuously—her eyes fell closed and open again. That softened gaze and a slackened scowl made her seem as pleasant as anyone while she savored the salt. And then the urban disdain returned.

With a fat pestle, the old woman mashed black fruit in two bowls.

"They grow it all along the Daughter," Cumalo said. The mounded berries spat dark juice, disintegrating into pulpy slurry. "Other than back home, I've never found it anywhere except in Mother of Waters." The tart musk of that aroma! "You can *bet* how surprised I was first time I saw it here." Men were meant, at this end of the continent, to eke out their tears. Demane therefore hardened his face against the surge of homesickness.

She unstoppered a jar. Hell and its chemicals scorched the air. "You boys take it with that Demon?"

"We good, we good!" Cumalo hurriedly assured her. "Sweet's just fine, ma'am."

She grunted and did not pour from the jar but set it aside. She scraped a mugful of dirty crystals from a sack. Half went to either bowl. The pestle worked the grit down into the indigo soup.

She stepped back and grunted once more. *You want em, get em.*

"Over there?" Cumalo nodded toward a prayerhouse, where northerners made petition to their fathergod. There about the entryway was the typical semicircle of wall, low and squat: just right for tall men to half sit, half stand.

"Hey now. You bring me *back* them bowls, hear?"

"Yes'm."

They perched on the balustrade. From within the prayerhouse emerged basso fulminations, and the muttered *amen* of lighter voices. *Sweet and credible are the lies of the Whisperer, enemy of God. So beware such close-close friendship, young brothers, lest Hell's dragon make you his plaything!*

Demane sipped. Every morning of a long romantic year—years ago now—Atahly had handed him bowls of crushed honeyed fruit, just a bit richer than this. And before then, his mother or father, or Saxa's parents, had fed him breakfast with the same. "How did she get it so sweet? That wasn't honey."

"*Sugar*, they call it. Down around Olorum they grow whole fields of the stuff as wide as kingdoms. Most goes overseas: up on the north continent, they can't get enough. You can't really find honey out this side of the continent. Nobody seems to know how to keep bees the way we do back home. Still, this tastes pretty good, I think." Cumalo looked at him as if fearing to see disappointment. "Or don't you like it?" Some youth arriving late to worship fled past them into the prayerhouse, casting the brothers a harried glance.

Demane sipped skeptically. "It's all right," he said grudgingly, but then couldn't hold back a huge grin. "Naw. It's good."

"See there? I *knew* you'd like it!"

They drank greedily and returned the bowls. Sat again outside the prayerhouse, Demane watched the flux of passersby, local and foreigner. He worked over in thought the same knotted frustrations as always: nothing coming loose, everything tightening.

Cumalo said, "Bossman's putting you through it, huh?"

Demane gave a bark of mirthless laughter, and said, *For he who is scaly, fanged and hornèd may breathe thusly into your ear, 'One lickle kiss; where's the harm?'* "What do you know of the gods, the Towers, and all that?"

Cumalo never looked fully awake, his eyes were so heavy-lidded. In fact, no one saw more, or more clearly. "Those are some deep mysteries right there, brother. You had to be initiated, over where I grew up. So all I really know is the same as everybody." Cumalo's speech grew incantatory: "The gods dwelled upon the earth." He pointed a finger at the dust. "The gods flew again to heaven"—pointing now to the sky—"and the gods did abandon their youngest born," pointing lastly at Demane, who nodded.

"Yeah, pretty much. As far as that goes."

"Why'd they do it, though?" Cumalo said. "Abandon y'all here? I always *did* wonder: the gods, just taking off into the great forever and beyond like that, and leaving behind their own children." You would have thought this man didn't have two sons and a baby daughter, fifteen hundred miles away and asking their mama right now, doubtless, *When's Papa coming home?*

"Exigencies of FTL," Demane answered. Distracted by a glimpse from the corners of his eyes, he lapsed into liturgical dialect. "Superluminal travel is noncorporeal: a body must become light." A tall, thin man passed by: some stranger, not the captain. "The gods could only carry away *Homo celestialis* with them, you see, because the angels had already learned to make their bodies light. But most *sapiens*—even those of us with fully expressed theogenetica—haven't yet attained the psionic phylogeny necessary to sublimnify the organism."

"No doubt." Cumalo nodded mellowly. "No doubt. I had always maybe *thought* it was something like that."

On the street before them a transient little drama arose and died.

That Demon rode a filthy derelict. Women in conversation scattered around the drunken man's floundering, doomsday rants, and selfsoiled stench. Once past him, the family of women came together again.

"Most people can't hold Him," Cumalo said sadly as someone who knew. "My advice, brother, is to let that Demon *alone*."

"I don't even mess with Him."

The grandmother, nieces, and aunties hadn't missed a word of their argument over the feastday menu, nor yet spilled onion, bound fowl, or gnarled tuber from their brimming baskets. And then the ruck of many black robes, and a corner turned, stole the view of importunate and accosted alike.

"Before the Assumption," Demane said, "the gods lived here on an island, in different Towers. We children only knew our own gods. My Aunty—my ancestor— came from Tower TSIMtsoa. Captain comes of another lineage, Ashé. Following me so far?"

"Uh huh. Go ahead."

"Coming down from my Tower, we're all aioloran-thropes—"

"Say again?"

"—*stormbirds*," Demane said, "thanks to the twenty-fourth chromosome. But in Tower Ashé the gods manipulated the genome another way, for polymorphism.

Some Ashëan . . . oh, you won't know what hyperpheno-types are; some *family-groups* are stronger and faster. The warriors. Some are smarter: the savants. Others are ora-cles and magi. I don't *know* all the Ashëan types. It's not my Tower. Back on the island, the family-groups served Ashé each according to their parasomatic strengths. Still with me?"

"Well, a couple words are flying a little high for me there, but I get you basically. You're saying, the captain comes from a line of warriors."

"No. I'm saying—" . . . *the mouth of the beast! Far better to fling yourself to wild lions, suffering the living flesh rent by tooth and claw, than that you should* . . . "—he *doesn't*," De-mane said. "I'm saying the captain was never meant for the fighting life at all. I'm pretty sure of it."

"Yeah?" Cumalo turned sleepy eyes on him. "You think so? Man's twice the warrior you are, and nobody else I ever met can take *you*."

"But that's just it, right there. You see what I mean? I'm no warrior either—"

"If the two of you aren't, it's got me wondering who in the Hell *is*."

"Come on, Cumalo! You know me better than that. Didn't my roots bind up the flux for you? And I pulled the poison out of that merchant's scorpion bite. You sat *watching me* sew Messed Up's face back on!"

"Yeah, all right. I see what you mean—a healer, then. And Captain's in the wrong life too. What's *he* supposed to be doing?"

Demane seized Cumalo's knee. "Hang on a moment, all right?"

Here came a plainsman with ruined ears and twice-broken nose, his broad-shouldered swagger cleaving through the crowd. In the freedom of that brother's wake strolled a much richer, smaller, older man, in robes the color of late dusk. Demane let go the knee and stood. "I'll be right back." Without meaning to, he came up to the strangers on their blind side, far too fast. The brother spun with clenched fists.

Their eyes met, and the feeling surprised them both.

Simpatico, sudden and bone-deep; ill will was impossible. There was a familiar quality about the brother's face. That aquiline nose ... was it someone Demane knew? And, hey—the brother had a nice smile, too. They nodded. Their hands joined, snapped apart, and rejoined, shaken in the manner of warriors well met hereabouts. Demane dragged his gaze to the merchant's.

"You doing all right, boss? I'm Demane," he said, "a brother with another caravan. I heard what you said back under the tower—"

"Kaffalah!" the merchant interrupted. "What is this man's purpose? Tell him I neither speak nor understand the rabble's cant." The merchant spoke in accents of Merqerim, westernmost of the coastal cities: not one of those Demane had yet visited.

"Kaffalah, brother." Demane turned back to the plainsman. "I just want to know if any of you seen what that lion look like. The color it was? My caravan, we leaving to go through the Wildeeps tomorrow."

The brother passed on these words to his master.

"The creature's color?" cried the merchant. "What *earthly* difference can that make? Tell this irrelevant fool that it was the king of monster lions! A rabid, man-eating tiger! Some unholy cat-fiend slipped the chains of Hell; a harrower of *men who fear God*, men who seek *but to fare the way* in safety, to earn an *honest living*! Color? Its color be *damned*! Did we not all hear the hellbeast roaring in the night? You tell him, Kaffalah. Tell him *this*! That if the greatwork on the Road has lost virtue, such that fell things maraud freely from the Wildeeps, devouring travelers at will, then that caravan which would go south by that route were *mad*. His caravan had better go west—yes!—even to the Great River itself, taking ferry for the far side, and traveling southward *thence*: outside the bounds of the Wildeeps. This man and his master count their lives as *nothing*, should they balk from such sweet wisdom as I speak now. There being no safety on the Road, it should bring them *joy* to bypass the

Wildeeps; yea, even to go *half a thousand* leagues off the direct route!"

A caravanmaster promises his merchants speed, safety, and thrift. Knowing this, now suppose some man comes whining to Master Suresh l'Merqerim. This man claims they must all take a months-long, budget-busting detour across the continent. Hmm, and on what basis? the master shall quite reasonably ask. Rumor and surmise, is the answer he receives. Well, says the master, extemporizing (for he considers himself a man of wide, deep wits, and so does not dismiss *any* counsel out of hand, but first weighs the credibility of his source); and whom does Master Suresh l'Merqerim find before him? What wild-eyed woebetider? Just a lowly guardsman—oh, *you* know the one! That so-called "Sorcerer" fellow, who hails from some green yonder off the very maps of civilization.

Demane's consternation was plain to see.

Kaffalah half-smiled. "You got all that, right?" He lifted his brows as if to say *Yeah, bruh: he be wearing me out too.* "It come in the night, so I never did see it myself. I just heard the roar a couple times. *Not* a lion, though I really couldn't tell you what. Like this—" The brother's jaw dropped: the merchant jumped, and the crowd nearby spooked en masse. Demane's flesh pebbled and chilled at Kaffalah's uncanny mimicry. "One brother did tangle

71

with it, and got chewed up pretty bad. Before he died, the brother said it was some kind of dark color. Not black. What he said . . ."—Kaffalah squinted and shook his head, acknowledging that his report could only be met with incredulity—" . . . that it was . . ."

"Green," Demane said in Merqerim; then, in his own tongue: *"Jukiere."* Cumalo came up and slung an arm over Demane's shoulder, nosily leaning in.

"Jooker?" Kaffalah said. "What's that?"

"You know!" Demane looked from Kaffalah to the merchant. *"Jukiere.* Big tooth, like lion, but only eat pork pork and . . . *we* pork."

The merchant frowned. "Speak sense, man. Who can understand what you are trying to say?"

Demane said, "Cumalo! What is their word for *jukiere?*"

"Jook-toothed tiger." Cumalo's Merqerim was excellent. "They are big cats and prey only on boar and people—they don't care which. Want a fresh kill *every* night, too."

"Jook-toothed tiger? The wizard cats? Do you mean the demons with teeth like this?" The merchant held an index finger curling down at either side of his mouth like outsized fangs. Briefly, he gave them a look of suspended disbelief, as one does when ready to laugh, provided the punchline proves good, and quickly forthcoming. Then the merchant became angry. "An old bush legend. Mere superstitious nonsense! There is no such thing as a *jook-toothed tiger*."

Ah, but there was. We, humanity, have our predators too, sir: and bred to the purpose. When the oceans swallowed the island, and the gods wicked and kind returned to heaven in their Towers, they left behind many children, powers that were benign and wrong, both. Among the worst were the wizard cats. The jukiere are clawed like lions, with teeth more terrible; as strong as bears, but wasteful and capricious killers, like polecats. And I've not yet spoken of their mastery of maleficia . . . in his own tongue, yes, Demane could have said all this and more. The best he could do in Merqerim, however: "Jooker, them . . . bad. *Bad* animal." He turned in frustration to Cumalo. "Will you please tell this fool that a *bush legend* ate up seven men from his caravan!"

Cumalo answered in Merqerim. "Maybe he's right, Sorcerer. I never heard of any jook-toothed tiger over here, this side of the continent."

The merchant had done with such folly. From already a few steps away: "Kaffalah!" He snapped his fingers as for a dog.

No mistaking the rapport went both ways. With surreptitious glances they'd made free of each other's person, and yet some strange reticence held as well: at least on one side. Kaffalah looked between Demane and Cumalo as if to suss out whether he came third where only two were wanted. Then, reluctantly, he said, "Take care, Dimani," and helped himself to a final good gander—from head to toe—for the road (only the briefest of nods to Cumalo). Letting go the hand he'd kept all this while, Kaffalah departed.

"Uh oh! What was all *that*?" Cumalo exclaimed. "I hope I wasn't breaking up your flow there, was I?"

"Aw, the brother was just being friendly, that's all." Demane shrugged off the arm. "Hey, Cumalo, listen. *We* came all the way across the continent, didn't we? A jukiere could too."

"You've been out here—what, two or three years? Brother, I came when I was *fifteen*, and I've been traveling ever since. In twenty years I never once saw or heard tale of any jukiere. It just doesn't seem too likely to me."

More than simians hate the serpent, stormbird and jukiere nursed ancient enmity. "Well," Demane said, "I'm going to let the captain know about it." In soul or flesh, some spark of primal fire seemed to take light in him. "Better to get off flat feet, and get out the knives, *before* the fight."—words Captain liked to say.

When youthful friends meet once more in vast old age, often they are astonished by the changes. But, of course, it wasn't age that Cumalo saw come suddenly over Demane's face. It was more weird than that, a far richer change. Somewhat wider-eyed than usual, Cumalo said, "Do what you think best, man. But you'd better *hope* it's no jook-toothed tiger roaming the Wildeeps."

"Why me? All of us had better hope ... Hey! I just thought of something." A mystery came clear in Demane's mind. "The captain has some plainsman's blood, I think. His nose is like that brother Kaffalah's. And isn't he sort of red-complected and brown all at once ... ?"

"If you say so." The look of alarm passed; Cumalo smiled. This was familiar ground, the enamored bending the conversation back again to his amour. "I don't see it, myself."

Teef thrust his head between theirs, slinging his arms across their shoulders. "You two cut out all that *ooga-ooga-bug-bug* over here." Which one worse: armpits or breath? Surely, the latter; but the unwashed inferno of his crotch and ass stank worst of all. "Y'all talk so a nigga could *understand*!"

T-Jawn, Barkeem, and the rest were with him. "Gotta jump, Cumalo," said a brother. "The dogs is done, and they setting up to put the cocks on next. You had said you wanted to lay a couple coins on the knife-birds. You coming?"

Cumalo looked at Demane. "You oughta come too. Might win you a little something."

"I'm good. Y'all go ahead." Demane got out from under the reeking arm. "I'ma go see about a bath over by Mother of Waters." He backed farther from the propinquities of funk. "Some brothers here might could stand one too."

"There go the Sorcerer." Teef shook his head, grinning that wrecked-tooth grin. "Always up in some damn water tryna *warsh*. Man, one day you gonna turn around, catch cold, and wake up dead behind all that water!"

Demane had tried to explain, in the caravan's early days, how the auspices of hygiene could ward off many infectious daemons. He'd wasted no end of breath laying out the basics of sanitary rites to the brothers. But all that dropped science had mostly bounced off their hard heads. A few kept clean, and the rest, well . . . "That ain't really how it work, Teef, but never mind," Demane said. "I catch up with y'all later."

Disputing groundbirds versus flyers, rash wagers versus acceptable odds, the brothers betook their stink and themselves up a northwest-running alley.

First, let it be understood that divinities crave tender companionship no less than we mortals do; thus enlightened, we may now begin to examine what form this tender companion of theirs ideally assumes: meet for the passions of a god, delightful to the heart and sensoria divine . . .

from Appendix H (Extinctions and Reemergent Taxa: *type, philomel*) of "Résumé of Ashëan Hyperphenotypes"; vol. 6, *The Olorumi Grimoire*

Third of Seven

He bathed in the Mother of Waters. Returning up the Mainway to the Station, he went this time into the warren of corrals and stables and warehouses, southside. Demane asked of a passerby, "Master Suresh l'Merqerim?" and found that name known. He had no problems following the directions.

Floor-to-ceiling shutters of the gallery above were folded back, and there, upstairs, the merchants reclined at a feast. On deep pillows, Master Suresh and his peers; on their knees, bowing again and again, servitors filled cups no sooner than they were drained. From mountainously heaped platters, merchants pinched up fingerfuls of rice ornate with cinnamon and cashews, charred yet tender bits of cabrito, rock salt and smashed garlic, dried apricots all moist and plump and soft again, onions turned to caramel ... Such were Demane's powers of scent and taste that he too partook of the meal, in every way except satisfaction. One of the merchants, if not Suresh himself, would now and again peer down from the gallery, on those busting their asses below, and find some cause to scream abuse.

Under the feast, workmen and the captain unpacked the camels' luggage, packed the burros' bags, rushed goods upstairs to be stored in one of three warehouses above the stables, and rushed down yet other goods to be squared away into the outgoing panniers. Captain hustled at his tasks as if his life depended on it. Taking perch on the corral's fence, Demane sat and watched. For a quarter of every night the captain lay as one dead, and the world's ending might not wake him. Otherwise, there were no idle moments for him. He ran on foot through the white-hot desert, though everyone else rode upon camels. He drilled himself at arms, or drilled the brothers. If he saw you working and the labors sufficed for two, he lent a hand; otherwise you got nudged aside. The man wore you out just looking at him.

Captain had changed his robe. He hardly smelled of himself, mostly of the aquifer minerals and endemica of Mother of Waters. Though never truly needing it, he'd gone to bathe as well. Ashëan idioviruses kept the captain's breath sweet, wounds sterile, and body odor, at worst, a musk that was sometimes a bit more peppery than usual. Had Faedou only obeyed, and allowed Captain to spit into that great gaping hole in his leg, as Demane had begged, then the wound wouldn't be festering, but healed nearly whole by now. "Good juju," however, had proved a poor translation for "panaceaic endosymbionts."

The work done, Captain gathered with the drudges around a water barrel, awaiting his turn to dip the ladle. Motion caught his eye: Demane jumping down from the fence. Captain handed off the ladle and started across the paddock. *Nothing's* better than your lover smiling to see you.

A shout fell on them from the sky.

"Skipping out, is it? This is how much your promises are worth? No more than a pig-raper's, set to watch the sty!" Master Suresh l'Merqerim leaned over the upstairs balustrade. "Who then will I get to—?"

Snarling, Captain spun and seized a barrel beside that from which the drudges drank. Was it empty? For he wrenched the barrel off the ground, and above his head, so easily. No—*half full*: weighing more than himself. Water cascaded from the open side as the barrel came up high and lateral—more splashing forth as it burst to staves and splinters against the side of the stable.

"Do you mind, Suresh? I'm coming right back." A brass quartet blasting ensemble might make such tuneful thunder.

Burros shied and neighed; the drudges, too. Everyone stared in astonishment, and none more so than Demane. Captain's anger was the cold kind, *never* hot.

Master Suresh l'Merqerim, mockingly, ducked as if dodging a wildly swung fist, and then left the balustrade to return to his feast.

Captain crossed to Demane. "Let's walk around here for a little bit." His whole organism exhaled the scents and signs of misery, of fury. "I don't have much time."

Demane nodded to the north. "Over by the Main-way?"

They vaulted the fence, went up the nearest alley.

"I should tell you something," the captain said. "I need to."

"Go 'head."

Demane glanced aside in time to see the familiar thing happening on Captain's face, his usual change of mind. Tensely parted, his lips were relaxing now. Whatever bold intimacy he had for one instant meant to confide would go unsaid after all, lost to habits of private endurance. Indeed as they walked, Captain said nothing at all. He picked at the edges of his headscarf, though of course no hair showed. The sun at zenith would have lit this alley all the way down to the dry packed dust. Now well after noon, oblique brightness crowned the captain's head, everything lower in shadow. Demane began to speak himself, telling of the encounter with the merchant, and what he suspected of the jukiere.

"A jook-toothed tiger, huh?" Captain, tiredly smiling,

shook his head. "Trust you to come at me with a story like that."

The cool dismissal stabbed right into the heart of any sense that they endured this ordeal together, as one. Did the captain have no confidence in Demane's expertise, did all the faith flow only one way? It hurt in the belly and chest to be brushed off so. Demane couldn't have guessed his own expression.

"A good thing you're always watching out. I'll say something to Suresh." Captain draped an arm across Demane's shoulders. "But if you think he'll change his plans on my say-so, you must have fallen and bumped your head." As the captain's hands could no more roughen with callus than they could scar, and bled every day, his thumb-pad and forefinger (playing with Demane's ear) were absurdly soft. "It'll just be the two of us looking out, as usual."

"Yeah." Demane swallowed and blinked. "All right." There'd never been anyone who could knife him so with a momentary word, and then speak the wound away in the very next moment. If all those little boyhood heartbreaks had been supposed to make him ready for this, Demane wasn't.

They'd nearly reached the sunwashed crowds ahead, when—seizing all Mother of Water's attention—the civil gong clashed to wake the dead. Men bawled in unison:

"Clear the Mainway! Clear the Mainway!" The alley was too narrow to admit either beasts or carts, but a stampede of pedestrians came running up its straits. Demane, smashed against the adobe of some stables, caught the captain, who was thrown bodily against him. An ugly moment, you would have thought, all the screaming and frenzied panic. But Demane had by now learned to recognize cover for a clinch, a pretext to grab two handfuls of ass. He stole that grope, the quick kiss collusive.

A drubbing ovation of horses at full gallop shook the earth. One thousand heads—and theirs, too—leaned out on the emptied Mainway. Twenty-five cavalrymen rode past, and onward through the Station-gates. The mounted fo-so, lances at the ready, ranged out along the east-west trail. Next, from the big western piazza, there came five men on foot. They were hunched over and terrified. Dogs—hacked-up carcasses—had been tied to them.

"Cheaters," said the captain. "They put poisoned collars on their fighting dogs." Packed into the alley were other refugees off the Mainway, and the eldest of a mother with more children than arms wriggled nearer: to hear the captain's song, and see what he glossed. "Or they fixed the odds, or else threw some match. Something like that."

Thicknecked mastiffs bibbed the men in front,

forepaws of the dogs wired at the men's napes, muzzles slobbering cold gore onto chins and chests. On top of rooves, at windows, and from the mouths of streets and alleys, Mother of Waters jeered.

The men ran up the Mainway. Hecklers flung offal, chucked stones.

"Anyone who makes the one-league waymark goes free." As in battle, Captain wore a look of bleak detachment. "No one ever makes it that far." To Demane's senses, the captain's mood seemed mostly enrapt attention, a little mixed with grief.

One of the indicted passed their alley—*booking*. His scentwake entirely fearsweat and adrenaline, this frontrunner doubled his distance from the rest every few steps.

Two others, neck and neck, lagged hindmost. One, a fat man, the other, thin but very old, staggered and lurched more than they ran.

Now a lone horseman emerged from the western piazza.

Captain murmured: "Fanged-drone."

Demane glanced at him. Above his beard, Captain brushed two fingertips down his own left cheek, scarless and smooth. (Though often wounded, he *had* no scars.) Demane looked back: the horseman's left-cheek insignia bore two stingers. Unlike the other calvarymen, he did not wield a lance, but viper of supple rawhide. Moaning like wind through arroyos, the serpent lashed the air about the horseman, in sinuous accord with his whirling arm. Spurred, his stallion surged forward. Mother of Waters cheered. Making no soft sound—*shrieking*—the snake unfurled to outpace sound itself for twenty feet. The viper kissed the runner midmost.

Bit him, rather: with a thunderclap.

"No, pop." Captain's forearms crossed Demane's chest like iron bars. "Stay with me." Captain reeled him back against long bones, hard scrawn. "You can't help them."

Demane, not even realizing, had moved to succor the stricken man.

The viper's bite had knocked Middle-Man to his knees. His scream was keening and breathless, nearly silent. His robe was split and gaping open—the shirt beneath as well, and living flesh, too. He reached one hand around his waist, the other over his shoulder, as if to catch some small swift thing nestling at his back. Just behind the man stricken, Fat-Man stumbled in astonished terror. He flopped belly down onto his passenger dog. Air currents moved such that Demane knew when Fat-Man's bladder voided. The wallowing man didn't and couldn't rise, flailing with the heavy stiff dog and swells of his own rolling suet, treading the hem of his robe. "Aw, that nigga *there*?" muttered some fellow-of-the-alley. "Bout to get *kilt.*"

Captain sang low. "There's no reason to watch, De-mane."

Yes, but how to look away?

The horseman pulled up short. (Breeze blowing northwesterly still: Fat-Man's bowels let go.) The one bitten clambered sobbing to his feet, a generous fillet peeling raw off his back, and struggled off after the old man who was passing the gates. Three times the viper bit the wallowing man. The first bite chunked out pudding from a wide thigh, laying white femur bare in grisly depths. There were screams, pleas, groveling. The next and deadly bite enwrapped Fat-Man's neck, hungrily gnawing through chins and jowls: crushing vertebrae with a splosive pop. So why then a third bite? Was it done to assure the crowd of a death, to show the body jolting up from the dust, only to fall again, still and silent? Was it done as a droll offering to the great demon, the antiurge, TSOA, that which incites human hearts to senseless evils? Yes.

Up reared the stallion! And how it *shone*, the breastplate of the rider! Nor with any lack of eloquence did the viper speak its single syllable, spoken in the very tongue of thunder. And the many hundreds who watched, what of them? Mother of Waters *roared*!

Demane had known noise in nature: he'd heard Mt. Bittersmoke erupt, heard white glaciers calving blue children; he'd stood once knee deep in mud beside his master, on the naked seabed, while she broke a hundred-foot whitewave of returning ocean, her pure will* slowing the apocalyptic waters—*such* noise!—but never before had Demane heard a thousand mortal voices compounding at full cry to deafen like some act of God.

Past the gates the cavalry could be seen distancing. With nimble pageantry, the corridor of lances raveled and rewove down the trail, hemming in the four runners still making dust.

Onward road the horseman and his viper!

Mother of Waters returned to business. Astride beasts, in vehicles, on foot, the crowd flooded the Mainway from tributary streets and alleys. Demane crouched down by the mouth of the alley, his back to a wall. A dizzying mix of the longing for home with the horrors of abroad made it impossible to keep his feet. "It's *ugly* here, Isa," Demane said, hanging his head between his knees. "How can you stand it?" Through the thickness of his

---

* That is, psychokinesis. Her wings beating: embubbled by her protection, and through the roiling aquatic chasm, he and Aunty came popping upwards into light and air. While he dogpaddled on the surface, she dragged herself airborne off turbulent chop. Then she plucked him from the waves, and flew them back toward the green hills, the undestroyed coast.

hair, rooting fingers found his scalp, the soft pads kneading. When Captain spoke so softly, and in this timbre, his speech was about as parsable as birdsong, more warble than words. Demane took comfort in the tone and intention, making no effort to decipher what was said. He resolved right then to go back to the green hills, just the moment after this man agreed to come too.

"This will be that Demon's work!" Master Suresh—jocund, rotund—came up the alleyway. "Taken by drink, is it?" The caravanmaster wagged a finger at Demane, who was crouched in the attitude of one inebriated. "They are *sots*, young man," scolded the master, "who would suckle Old Nick's bitchy teats so much, so early in the day!" To the captain: "About time, isn't it? Oh yes, indeed: so let's gitty up, Cap'n!" Master Suresh swept by them in his silks.

Demane made himself stand (the hand in his hair long since whipped away).

"See you tomorrow, all right?" The captain offered a counterfeit smile. "Keep the brothers out of trouble for me." Nerves and shame were embittering his wonted scent, as if, against honest instincts, Captain were trying to pull over a con—say, to sell twice, to different men, some singular treasure.

Demane looked from the captain to Master Suresh, who was stepping onto the Mainway. Not a comely man, nor kind, either; he was fabulously rich, though, and dressed in the bright-dyed shit of worms. Demane's guts sickened, on fire. He turned back to Captain, making the same face men betrayed in love have always made.

"*No,*" Captain whispered. "Don't even think it." Somehow, this denial was true, for Demane could spot even dissembling and misdirection. "It's like I told you before." *Until you there's been nobody, all my years on the road.* And how old was the captain, anyway? About thirty, to the eyes and senses; but . . . the blood-of-heaven ran very pure in him, as it had in Aunty. Although millenarian, she too had smelled confusingly ageless, "about thirty."

"What's going on here, Isa?"

"I've got to go," Captain said. "I'm tired of running. And don't follow, Demane, or I'll let death catch me." Here was more truth, and the captain had never yet said to him anything truer, or more heartfelt.

They jumped at a dry-stick report. Master Suresh beckoned. Impatiently, he snapped his fingers again. Captain went. He and the master crossed the Mainway, then walked up a northwestrunning alley. Fo-so were hefting the bodies of man and dog into a cart.

A storm was rising in the blood that pumped wildly through Demane. He couldn't hear his own thoughts, could hardly think them. *Run,* since he couldn't fly. Perform some worthy feat. A feat as hard and perilous as possible. *Kill something.* He too went out on the Mainway—but eastward through the gates, and then south toward the jukiere and Wildeeps.

———————————

There is a pace that a fit man can hold, running on and on, nearly forever. The sun westered slowly across the wide afternoon sky. South of Mother of Waters, there was rocky country through which a millennium of caravans had blazed a trail winding far from the Daughter, down shallower stretches of deep-cut arroyos, around high mesas, across scrub flats. This was neither the season nor perhaps the year that rains would fall; only the intermittent green of sagebrush, pampas, and acacia relieved the droughted shades of gray and dun.

Demane at first heard and smelled little more than anyone would. The pounding and raised dust of his own footfalls, mesquite hanging in the hot air, calls of mourning doves and cicada. Then the vacant hush of human perception began to fill with bright effigies of sound and odor. What was long passed, what was hidden, what was remote came clear to his senses.

A subtle roar built of discrete sounds. The stormbird heard insectskitter and the slide of snakes over stone. He felt it, wind too faint for his skin to feel before, and heard it, rasping particles of dust across the hardpan. The dazzle of scents bloomed. He passed the cold acridity of gecko, and rattler, and ground croc. Old bones murmured stories to him in passing. A child mummifying beneath a wayside cairn: dead of blood cancer. Manifold dung and urine, steer men lion antelope dog, whispered what age and sex, sick or healthy, how long since passing this way.

Faraway some early night dog barked. He'd seen the packs harry a solitary lion or stag antelope in the prime of strength, scores of muzzles stripping the prey of its fleshly raiment, gobbet by mouthful, and sacrificing ten or more dogs to immense antlers, or the might of a lion's paw, before the better beast was pulled down by sheer rabid numbers. Demane masked his body's odor in the landscape's, as he should have done at the gates of Mother of Waters. He quit the beaten trail and ran upcountry, where the lookout and cover were better.

The stormbird beat nearer the surface than it had ever risen—even on sacred grounds back home, in the green hills. He ran harder. His legs and lungs refused to tire. Strength and sensation swamped the indweller, that part of consciousness which thinks and feels. *I hardly ate today* were the last words to trouble his mind for a while. He was ravenous. And below him on the blazed trail, hidden in thick tamarisk, he caught the tattoo of a thumb-sized heart pumping frantic blood. The rich scent came too, of a small shivering body, furred and hot. There was good food just out of sight, a jack-hare about to lose its wager whether to run or hide. In that tussock of weeds right . . . *there* . . .

Buoyant on spirals of warmth. There athwart the west snaked the Daughter, glittering gray, and down there the southern Crossings, a thicker python, wider waters. He plunged into fresh headwinds. In his shadow stampeding antelope small as crickets separated in the same patternly accord as a birdflock, scores bounding left, scores right, through blond grasses that rippled over the world's skin. Aw, let them go. He wasn't so hungry anymore. Better to ride more soft rising heat up where . . . where, exactly? The skyfaring dream came to ground. Every tremor of his lids and lashes abraded the dream's stuff, and his eyes opening destroyed it.

Fast water sloshed over him, rocking him. Legs outstretched, leaning back on his elbows, Demane awoke in the shoals of a broad stream, wallowing. His bag hung submerged in the current. Panicked, he jumped up. The bag's flap was thrown back, but water hadn't entered. Wetness sheeted from the leather and it was dry again in moments. Nothing within was out of place. Aunty used to say, Don't worry so much: the bag takes care of itself. She had always laughed at his fretful care. Wasn't it better, though, to err on caution's side?

And stretching before him was the Wildeeps. Across stream, rich as the rainwoods back home, tangled ancient growth went on and on, green to the east and west horizons. The oceanic foliage rippled and petals like white tongues blew down. The whole southern bank of leafage tossed in gusts of wind which, midstream, Demane felt only as soft breath, scented with frangipani.

And the ground over there was sacred, the jungle godlike and consecrated only to itself. A greatwork lay over the stream where he stood, and over the fast water running on all frontiers of the Wildeeps. Demane laughed. He ran for high steps through the rapids, and crouched down, to swing an open hand against the water's rush and knock up white splashes. The two greatest wonders of his life, both together at once: one of nature, the Wildeeps where many worlds overlapped; and another wonder, this artifice of magi, the greatwork that bound this savage country and its denizens.

Downstream, he saw a weird pulsing light, stationary just above the trees. Demane waded with the flow, west.

Nude black dirt, a southrunning trail, cut into the greenery across stream. Some bright sign—a thunderbolt, caught and twisted by almighty hands—hovered coruscating at treetop-height over the mouth of the trail. Demane knew what amounted to a library's worth of dis-

parate lore, and all of it word-perfect, though he was il-
literate in the four languages he spoke. Still, that brightness in the sky was legible to his very blood. It read, *Here
is the Safe Road*. Eyes closed, his face could find the folded lightning and know its meaning too, even as the blind
feel upon their faces where the sun sits in the sky.

The hard current dragged and eddied about his feet.
Demane shuddered, and looked bewilderedly around
him, coming fully alert like a slapped sleepwalker.

What had he meant to do, exactly? Track the jukiere
across the Wildeeps, kill the wizard somehow, and then
return to Mother of Waters, all in one slender evening—
was that the plan, then? *No*, of course not! He'd only
wanted to . . . scout out the lay of the land. Ye-ah. That
made some kind of sense.

Well, brave scout, will you look at the hour? In the
west one low cloud glowed sullen and red, its underbelly
brass-bright. The blue dusk was blackening, the sun already below the horizon. Perfect nightvision had let the
dark creep up on him again. Demane recalled some little
animal in the grass. And he'd . . . killed it? And then what?
Not *eaten* it, surely, had he? How? His spear, blades, and
bow were all untouched in the bag. Running his tongue
(not leathery and rough, but a soft fragile slug, like anyone's) over his teeth: they were all blunt, not mostly
pointed ivory tines. He examined his hands. Quarter-

moon talons, keen-edged as scimitars along the under-
sides? Since when? *Of course* there were ordinary human
nails at the tips of his fingers. He shrugged: nor did any
strange new muscles move in his back. He was wingless.
Some half-fledged potential stirred in him, though. Lim-
itless and untapped, the wellspring of the Wildeeps
awaited the one who would drink. So close to the
Wildeeps, nothing was beyond achieving if only Demane
would cease to hold himself back so fiercely. *And is that
what you still want, no longer to be a man but a god . . . ?* He
spun around and ran for the north bank of the fords. He
fled back toward Mother of Waters.

It was as though a great wind carried him across that
first leg upcountry, not any strength of his own. But the
Wildeeps dropped leagues behind, and the stormbird
waned. Fatigue began to drag at his legs and Demane
slackened from his best pace to one he could hold. The
slow air momentarily strengthened to a breeze. Very
nearby, in the dark above the trail, a night dog bayed. In a
sweat of sage musk, green attar, and chlorophyll, Demane
expunged his scent; but it was too late. The pack had sight
and sound of him. Coursing and unshakeable, a score of
dogs set up frenzied barking. Demane fled without any
plan except to live longer, his feet quickening again.

Dogs run much faster, however, and soon closed the
distance. He had to turn and face them. Six in front all

but snapping at his heels leapt, jowls foaming, teeth sharp. Time left him again. Coming to he spat a foul mouthful of furred meat. Doubtfully he tottered, nodding with unfocused eyes. Aching up and down his arms and legs: the print of savage bites which hadn't broken skin. Limbs and carcasses strew the churned mud about him, his hands gloved in blood. He needed food—cooked, spiced, *vegetable*. Hunger had drawn his stomach tight as a fist.

Demane spat again, a thirsty paste, and began to run. There was a stitch under his ribs, cramps in his thighs, and fatigue that made him wish to lie down anywhere. But he wouldn't survive another attack, and so step after step, his scent belatedly hidden, he ran on through the starblown night.

Human noise and stink wafted toward him across the drylands. The Station glowed in the distance. Ahead on the trail, barking, savage and remote, addressed some other prey; Demane had to detour far and wide. Meanwhile the moon's jaundiced eye wandered half its nightly course across heaven. The gates at the tower stood closed.

He circled west to the lake, and washed away the muck and dust. With his legs turning hard and stiff, Demane gimped up the Mainway from Mother of Waters. Fatty smoke from barbecue and his roaring hunger pulled him through the glad crush of the Station's night crowd, and then down a street above the revels on the piazza. He walked past every grill to a particular fellow, turning a haunch over spluttering coals. "Fresh!" said the man, full of pride, grinning at Demane. "Killed it just this evening, not long ago!"

Demane knew that, *smelled* it, and made his order.

He kept his eyes squinted, for the more sensitive the nightvision, the more cruel the artificial lights of civilization. On a dish of unfired clay the grillmen handed Demane: mashed yam, half charred tips of rare beef, once-tough greens tender from long simmering in pot liquor. Demane set the dish on the ground and tore a withered pepper over top, spilling pale seeds. He rasped two little saltrocks together, dusting the food thoroughly, and handed up both pieces to the vendor, who smiled again. The grillman turned to serve another.

"How you all do *complicate* the thing! Yes, there is the problem of witches: whether they be stronger than natural men, dodging blows which should have landed, or exploiting other such fraudulent advantages. But only think for a moment. Every one of us knows perfectly well what a proper fight looks like. A man who wins legitimately comes up from his descent into the pit *spitting blood*, staggering, hard-used, *hideous to see. And where is there the creature to take such a battering an he need not?* He, however, who passes unscathed from bout to bout—making easy mince of formidable opponents—*that man* is a witch! Watch for him! Let's not overcomplicate the matter. To catch a witch-cheater needs nothing more than to keep our eyes peeled . . ."

His Excellency Sabiq bgm Qaby, Royal-cousin, speaking to fellow trustees of the Fighthouse at Mother of Waters

Fourth of Seven

A town like no other in his experience, the Station at Mother of Waters, where noise and business picked *up* after dark. There were more people on the piazza than all the men, women, and children living in Demane's hometown, whose houses spread out over three hills, the farthest families a whole morning's walk away. He came upon Faedou sitting on the margins of the piazza. He had a jar beside him, his bad leg stretched along a wall, out from under the feet of enraptured dancers or the blundering Demonridden. Demane pressed one hand flat to the wall, leaned heavily, and worked his sore legs down to sitting. But he'd hardly got settled and halfway comfortable before Cumalo came out of the crowd.

"Sorcerer!" Cumalo's fingertips tapped upon the air, playing invisible beats. "Get my drum out for me, will you? The good one. I want to play!"

"All right." Demane fought laboriously to standing. "Be right back." He looked for a corner out of the good light, hidden.

"Aw, man, *come on*! Why you going off somewheres?

Just pull it out of your bag right here. Nobody cares!" Cumalo danced, hands busily pantomiming. Miracles didn't seem to faze him. What a strange, wonderful town *he'd* come from! Demane's own mother, father, and siblings used to avert their eyes, sneering in terror, at the smallest miracle—to say nothing of these superstitious northerners!

"Can't do that, brother. I'll be right back."

Down between two inns bordering the piazza, there was a cul-de-sac that ended against a remnant of the old fortwall. Where men had pissed out that Demon since before the fall of Daluça, Demane stooped in ammonia shadows and felt around in his bag. The drums were in the back bottom hall, past tarp and tent, surgical kit and medicines, food and sealed jars of pure water, knives, bow and arrows, his spear, various leather saddles, for dromedary and equus . . . ay, Aunty! Would you scold or laugh—shocked, either way—to see the bag so messy, things spread out everywhere? He found Cumalo's jimbay and pulled it forth. Back in brightness around the greatorch, Demane handed the drum over. Cumalo joined the twenty or so others playing.

The moment Cumalo lit into the opening evolutions of a hotter, faster rhythm, the other drummers fell in behind his mastery. "The *old* music," Demane said, throwing up a palm in excitement. "That's some *church* he playing!" Dozens talking, dozens standing, rushed out to join the hundreds who danced. The crowd jumped like waterdrops flicked onto a hot greased griddle. How to sit out this joyful noise, the spirit so willing! But the body begged to stay put.

"Well, go dance, then!" Faedou waved him up. "Thought *you* would of been out there, if anybody."

Demane grinned and shook his head. "I'm getting old, old man."

Faedou blew like a horse. "Boy, I got two sons and a daughter older'n you."

Maybe just stand up and shuffle a little, at least? He reached back to push off the wall and began to raise up, but his own abused flesh fought the unfolding of his legs with such ferocity, all stiff and chilled, Demane lost heart and settled back down sitting.

"Cut out all that groaning!" Faedou hooted. He drank from his jar. "You sound worse than me!"

A waif appeared, and stood by patiently. Faedou gulped the dregs from his jar and handed it up. The child sped away, and then with slow careful steps returned, bearing back the jar brimful.

Demane asked, "How's that leg doing you?"

"Same way it's *been* doing," Faedou said. "Let me be, Sorcerer. I ain't in no kind of mood to talk about it."

So they talked of the road ahead. About as many

leagues farther to the south as they'd already come, Great
Olorum sprawled on the Gulf. It was a kingdom of many
principalities grown together into the vastest of cities,
none bigger in the world. And close by Olorum, Faedou
said, could be found an outpost of heaven where seven-
foot giants lived, supposedly the children of the gods. *The
Ashëan Enclave*, Demane thought but did not say. More
edifying to listen, he had learned. He tried to square the
science Aunty had taught him with Faedou's superstitious account, all gilded with legend and rumor. There
being no god but God, said the old man, those tall folk
could hardly be his special children, now, could they?
They surely were a sight to behold, though. The naps
growing *blue* on their heads, if you could believe it; and
hair that glimmered like the sunplay of precious stones
handled in bright sunlight. And what were they called,
anyway, the blue ones . . . ?

"Em'ralds?" Demane put forward.

"No, man: wrong one! I mean the other'n. *Blue.*"

Faedou swore up and down that he'd once seen such
a sky-coiffed man, passing through the far crowd: taller
even than the captain, and his hair like cobwebs, with the
refractive lucency of . . . those blue rocks.

"Rubies?"

"*No!*"

Every day of his life until today, Demane had grieved

to be born so late a grandchild of TSIMTSOA, so many mortal generations from his divine progenitor, that there was small hope of ever attaining the glories of the storm-bird. He'd failed to give much thought, however, to problems facing cousins born of the other Towers. Suppose you *didn't* have two faces, one mundane, one miraculous, but just a singular that combined both qualities? Then you'd have to go through life revealing all your secrets to whoever threw you a glance. That, or else be fretting every moment of every day over some tightly wrapped headscarf... And yet, to *eat* stellar radiance! What does a sunrise taste of? Not the same as starlight, surely. And the equatorial sun at noon? (Remember these thoughts: *ask him.*) Suppose that gross food altogether were something you could take or leave, like hot peppers, or sweets? *Oh, thank you, but no: just this sublimity of light's enough for me.* Someday* Demane would like to examine the heliophages of Captain's scalp carefully, up close. The curly wires on his chin and chest and so forth were darkest

---

* Of all words, none more purely distills the futility of human hope, mortal dreams. Did we but know the end is foreordained and soon, who could go on making such tender plans—*someday I shall run my fingers through my lover's hair*—when the very next step we take shall pitch us into the sinkhole, there to be crushed to nothingness, smothered in an instant, by a thousand tonnes of earth? "Someday." *Ha!*

brown, a little chestnut, a little fawn intermingled, and one or two strands the vivid shade of the setting sun halved at the horizon—

"Son, you doing all right over there?"

"Mm, what happen?" said Demane. He looked around, rallying back to the here and now.

"Seem like I lost you there, for a moment. You feel all right?"

"Yeah, Faedou. Naw, I'm listening." Demane banged a fist on his thigh, waking up dormant aches, getting his thoughts back on path. "So what about 'sapphire'? Zat what the blue one called?"

Nine or ten brothers drifted off the piazza to sit with them and talk the night out, the morning in. The adept spends a long time under tuition, but none of his studies readies him, afterwards, for the loud surmise of men in fellowship, each one shouting genial ignorance at his fellows. Mostly, Demane could nod and smile, laughing when the others laughed. Kazza, who was a fount for the songs and customs of diverse peoples, objected when someone's guesses ranged too far off the mark.

"No, that's not why! It's the *old way* in Sea-john, where he's from. Men and women there, they only bare their heads for a lover. For husband or wife. Don't you just love that? I love it! So romantic. That's why Captain never takes that scarf off."

"El capitán got him a woman somewhere?" Wilfredo looked around to see who knew. "¿Ehtá casao?"

"Won't you just ask'im, Willy?" Cumalo urged in his lazy drawl. "You know it ain't nothing the captain love better than some newzy-ass sumbitch all up in his business."

Demane laughed loudest of all. He hadn't known that Sea-john custom!

Faedou changed his mind which wife he loved better; here, tonight, drunk: "the Old Girl." So many in the telling were his first wife's charms, it was hard to see how "the Little Missus" had ever got ahead in his affections, even for a little while. Other men spoke of their wives, and brothers of women they hoped to marry; and when the theme was passed to Demane, he spoke too.

"We do it another way where I come from," he said. "The lady choose for herself. And my Atahly, her mother was—I guess you say, here—*king*. The chief? That's why Atahly could do whatever she want, have any man. She said, let me try you, Demane, for a year or two, then maybe we marry."

"You two have a baby, Sorcerer?"

"No." Though there would be one by now, surely. Sucking a tiny thumb, other hand grabbed in mama's skirts: a sturdy baby girl, maybe, toddling after her lovely mother; not Demane's daughter, though. "Stay and marry me, Atahly said. *Then* a baby. But I left."

"Ain't you suppose to be the smart one here, Sorcerer?" said Faried. "I would of married a girl like that! How could you just up and leave?"

"Baby, looking at y'all ugly face everyday, I wonder sometime too."

Kazza had a nose for sad romance. "You ever love anybody else, Sorcerer?"

"Oh, sure. For a long time before me and Atahly got together."

"What happened? What was *her* name?"

His name was Saxa. "It's a whole long story." Demane sighed.

The night then began its descent, down and down, to become the ugliest yet of Demane's life.

There came fetching up from the flooded piazza another noisy bunch of brothers, T-Jawn, Barkeem, Teef: that whole rough crew. They were on fire about what had just gone down at the Fighthouse: "Niggas was smashed up in there 'til you couldn't *move*." "Hot like midday up in the desert." "Everybody screaming they *head* off!" Telling the tale, the brothers passed a triplesize Demoniac jar from hand to hand, drinking thirstily.

Barkeem: "Why y'all didn't come? Should of *seen* that shit!" The captain, it seemed, had fought seven men, one after the next, and "knocked" (Teef speaking) "err last one of em out." "Mais hélas" (T-Jawn) the captain was so well known at the Fighthouse, odds had been set at 50/1; nor could all Master Suresh's guardsmen together have produced the fifty silver pennies necessary to make a wager. "Yeah, but" (another brother) the caravanmaster and four or five of those other merchants had put down "crazy money on the captain. *Them* motherfuckers made out like BANDITS."

In gore-soaked detail they recounted the casualties of Captain's clean sweep. A man's pulped nose, another's mouthful of shattered teeth. Yet some other man who, shoulder wrenched from its socket and twisted up his back, had screamed *Mama*. A man's eye burst to jelly in its socket. A hand stomped, the fingers limp as raw calamari. Knee wrong way back. Sudden silly swooning fall.

"Captain was a MONSTER." The five come from the Fighthouse all agreed no other word suited: *Monster*, they said several times praisefully, eyes ashine, heads nodding. They would persuade all who'd missed the show of this truth: *what* a monster!

"Hoshit, though! Y'all remember that next-to-last one?"

"Yeah, *he* could fight. Knocked Captain down *twice!*"

"None of them other niggas lasted as long as that one. Didn't y'all think... was a *little* while there, I thought Captain might be gon' lose. Bossman was looking *tore-*

down that second time he got up."

Oh, sorry, says your lover to you. *Can't tonight; I've other business!* So what's he doing then? The man is maiming seven weaker men, that's what: this, for the captain, being the most delightful of all ways to pass the first free night they'd had in months. Oh, and let's not forget that—according to eyewitnesses—he killed at least one of those seven. *Killed a man.* And for what? For sport, for lucre. Not in self-defense, not to save a friend, but murder in pursuit of the shiny trash-metals that civilization prized more highly than human life. *Tell us, my son: how are you faring in those strange lands, so far from home? We your parents do so often think of you and worry. Whom have you chosen to walk with, to talk to: some good woman, some kind man?* Nothing Demane had ever felt, no past high or low, could match the intensity of his frustration then. Such emotion needed an out. Yes: other heads were about to feel this balked love as a rain of fire. For such virile alchemy was commonplace in those parts, at that time: there, with wearisome ease, the men could turn private pain into public fury.

"He *won*, though. And GotDAMN! Y'all *seen* how Captain kicked that brother, at the end? So the man *jaw* drop off his face, onto his chest? Then stomped that nigga when he down?"

"Yo, I heard em say: Captain broke dude's back! Just

broke it. Couple of them barber-surgeons they had up in there was saying, wasn't *no way* brother was gon' make it through the night."

"Nor even so long; that soul has already flown. I did linger to watch, me, after you lot rushed out—*fiending*, that's the word, n'est-ce pas?—to suck upon that Demon's poisoned cock. (I say there, White Boy! Are the rest of us meant to perish of thirst, then? All the niggers who sit to your left? *MER*de! Let's have those evil spirits passed *this way* too!) The chirurgeons of the Fighthouse could do nothing for the man. He died. But not before taking all manner of fits. *Comme ça.*" T-Jawn feigned grand mal: limbs aflail, foaming at the mouth, head flung back, eyes bugged and rolling in their sockets.

"Ha ha! You *stupid*, Jawny. Why you so damn crazy?"

"Wait, wait. Which one was that? Big plainsman motherfucker, with the jacked-up ears? Nose coulda been broke like ten, twelve times? That brother—wossname—*Kafflay* or some shit?"

"Yeah, fool. Who your dumb-ass THINK we talking about?"

"Y'all," said Cumalo. "Come on now, y'all. Simmer down some. You finna make him mad."

"Who mad? But for real, Sorcerer. You shoulda been there! That was some sure 'nough *shit* you missed, my nigga!"

Demane blazed up like a dry thatched roof. "Didn't I say DON'T BE CALLING ME THAT." Biggest anyway, he shot to his feet in the seated gathering. He meant just to kick the jar from Barkeem's hands; the cheap crockery exploded.

Barkeem curled up on his side, a fetus, or exposed bug. "Please," he said, and, "I'm sorry!" asking, "What I do? What I do?" One hand he stretched out to soak up the force of any falling blow; the other arm he curled round his head, for a helmet against kicks. Just a year had passed since Barkeem had fled his father's house, and the sudden furies racking it; sixteen long years he'd lived in that hell. That Demon soaked his robes.

"Get outta here, all y'all," Demane said to those come from the Fighthouse. "I don't wanna *hear* no more!" Barkeem wasn't wrong: there'd be fists and stomps for any slow to take their heels. But, as no one there had ever seen the Sorcerer enraged, they all sat gaping. "GO!" Demane lunged and five brothers scrambled up and away. One not fast enough: White Boy caught a foot to the backside. That kick, with a yelp and three huge staggering steps, sent the brother veering off into some dancer's embrace, who at once shoved him away. He fell sprawling.

At one time or another, from sickness, or wound, or other misery, Demane had succored them all. And so those five brothers—astounded by this abuse without precedent—wheeled around in confusion, right nearby: doublechecking that Demane and this mad stranger were truly one and the same. He snarled and balled his fists. "*Get* y'all dusty tails away from here."

They slunk off.

"Dang, Sorcerer," said Kazza. "You scared them bad." Scared himself, it was clear, by the wary awe with which he watched for the big man's next act.

Fuck them niggas. "They be all right," Demane said. And his body all charged with righteous violence, but the villain nowhere in sight, he swung his heavy arms out and jerked them back in, banging his own chest once with each fist. Captain had destroyed *seven men*, one of them *dead*. And what shape would the monster be in himself; all bloody and bruised now, torn and staggering?

"Somebody here"—Demane squinted around painfully, the greatorch at center-piazza dazzling his nightvision—"point me to the Fighthouse." It was one of those cubic hulks looming on the piazza's northwest peripheries, wasn't it? Or a block or two farther north?

"Nah." Faedou shook his head. "You don't need to go over there." He patted the ground. "How about you set right back down, instead."

"Captain . . ."

" . . . ain't studn you, Sorcerer. He don't need, damn sure don't *want*, none of your do-gooding, witchcrafting help. What Captain would appreciate round about now is some peace and quiet, to be sick and in pain all by hisself. That's how he was the last six times we come through Mother of Waters. I figure he that same way tonight. Would probably knock your head off, you come near him right now. So might as well just set right back on down where it was you got up from."

Demane looked around him in befuddlement, and the brothers stared back. The sweep of his gaze came to rest on a brother in particular: "*You* knew he was going to the Fighthouse tonight." Cumalo's mouth dropped open, but he got no sound out, only sat gobbling. "*Why didn't you tell me?*"

"Hey there," called Faedou. "Hey now. Before you go shouting whatever you shouting at your homeboy Cumalo, you *might* wanna hear the reason why the captain done it."

"Why he done it?" Demane shouted. "Ain't no reason why, old man! Captain took a mean cold look around him, and figured the world could use five or six more cripples, and a couple dead dudes on top. So he says, hows about I get myself down to the *Fighthouse*, see what I can *do* about this. Earn me some full-boys, too."

"No, son. And it really gotta be said—I ain't never *seenchu* so out your right mind and good sense. You just as wrong as you wanna be." Faedou lifted his jar between both hands prayerfully, fortified himself deeply, and then sighed. "*Sure* you don't wanna hear why he done it? I hold the man in some esteem and admiration, myself."

Pricked already by intimations of his own foolishness, Demane doubled down, and puffed out his chest. "Well, why then?"

"Set."

Demane didn't sit. And then slowly, very stiffly, he did.

"Your first time crossing down to Olorum, ain't it?"

They all knew it was. Why ask?

"Cause I'ma give you something to think about," said Faedou. Here at Mother of Waters, the caravan had just reached the halfway point, with already six brothers bandit-killed out of twenty-five starting out. They still had the Wildeeps to go, and the endless prairies; and past those, eight or nine days in the monkey forests just north of the Kingdom, and there, under the trees, the desperados just about *ruled*, ever since the death of the great prince, called the Lion of Olorum; ever since the old King had slipped into his final senility. Other caravanmasters paid their guardsmen five silver full-weights, *seven* if you were lucky. With a little scuffle and thrift, a man could keep a wife and baby fed, under a roof, and in clothes for two or three years on a half dozen full-weights. But a lot of brothers were carrying *much* more family than that. So this here caravan wasn't some sight-seeing jaunt across the continent for them. The whole fortunes of families, from greatgrands to great-grandchildren, hung in the balance.

"You ain't heard what I said, so let me say it again? For all that distance, all that danger, most brothers just get peanuts: six silver full-boys."

Now did you ever stop and wonder why *this* caravan, out of all of them, paid so much? Master Suresh was going to open up a sack *loaded down* with silver and let each brother take a good grab out. A small hand could pull out ten or twelve full-boys *easy*. Big-ass ones like Demane's? Might get up to *twenty*. So why in the Hell was Master Suresh paying that much? Where all that damn money coming from? Who—care to guess *who*, Mister Sorcer-er—had put up his own life in the Fighthouse of Mother of Waters, just so those greasy fat-cat money-bags could make them a killing, and some the sweet juice of that haul could trickle down to the brothers? "So then. Tell me *now* what you gotta say for yourself, all big and bad?"

Nothing; for a long moment Demane sat contemplating the juncture of his crossed legs, his empty hands resting there, feeling the heart chewed up and spat back into his chest, and then looked up.

"Let me get a sip of that, what you drinking."

"Aw, son." Faedou shook his head. "That Demon don't

fix nothing. You too good for this shit."

"No, I ain't." Demane reached out a hand. "Let me try some."

"Son, I'm *telling* you."

"Pass me that jar, old man."

In prurient anticipation of disaster, ten brothers leaned as one to watch when Faedou handed over the jar. Demane lifted it and sniffed. Elsewhere in the world, one cur of a famished pack was sniffing at strychnined meat, and suffering the very same qualms as Demane. *Poison*, said these fumes; but look at all the others partaking. Was it not primitive and backcountry, then, always to be trusting one's own senses? Thus, even forewarned, dog ate, man drank. Bad water in a ditch where geese, crossing the continent, alit to crap, bears stopped to piss, and up through which foul gas, clots of oil, were burbling from the green sludge of the bottom; and this whole foul brew—thanks to a storm last night, some lightning strike—set *on fire* . . . That Demon was so much worse than this. Demane gagged. He wheezed breath in. He hacked it back out.

Brothers fell out laughing.

Faedou retrieved his jar. Cumalo beat upon his brother's back. "Told you not to be messing with it." Hangdog and gasping, Demane could only cough upon his knees and shake his sorry head. Which he lifted up, as some fresh stir moved through the gathered brotherhood.

"By the Holy Recital of Life and Days, looky here," said old Faedou, eyes on the piazza's crowd. "Bet your ass, this is some trouble coming." Brothers with backs to the view turned around, Demane among them. "Here come the king and prince of chuckleheads, bringing us some news. Ain't no good news, though! *Watch.*"

It was Xho Xho and Walead, at a dead run. "Yo! Yo! Sorcerer!" The boys were beside themselves. "So this man. This bad man? This man we had ran into, right? He sold Messed Up some *qaïf.*" So wicked and busy a fellow is This Man We Had Ran Into! Has anyone else ever stirred up such trouble across all worlds, from the deepest past to the very days we are living in? "So then, Messed Up was *smoking* with dude, right?" But not, one could hardly fail to note, smoking alone. For a mighty funk of burnt herb had come wafting in with Xho Xho and Walead, and their eyes were droopy, awfully blood-shot. "It was that good shit, Sorcerer. Everything, *chill.* So then why did dude have to just *up and say* something to Messed Up like that? You *know* Messed Up don't be try-na hear it! Now that nigga STRAIGHT BUGGING. Yo, Sorcerer, you gotta come *quick*—fore Captain or the fo-so get him!"

Having just set the house on fire, two boys would raise the alarm with this same whine and dance. Demane let himself be pulled up and dragged (a skinny brother at each hand) through the riotous boogie and bounce on the piazza. Coming and going in the heatless glare of the greatorch, his sight was a sometime thing. Every other brother, of course, pushed along through the revels too, all save their eldest, lame and dying.

Conjoined in violence to the familiar gargantua, a little stranger fought to free himself. Messed Up righthandedly flung about and shook his most unwilling detainee, while lefthandedly trying to inflict fatal damage on another—any other—from the usual heckling monkeyhouse of fightwatchers.

The wrappings of Messed Up's loincloth showed, his robe was so far ripped down. Teeth had worried his right forearm to gruesome effect. Nose freshly pulped, the face of This Man We Had Ran Into was a monster mask of blackslimed teeth. Messed Up screamed pure madness.

"Ahm bout to WHOOP somebody ass! Who else want some? You? *You*, then? How come y'all running—*stop running*! Ain't NOBODY here wont they ass whoop? Awls ah see is a buncha scaredycat jumpback turntail COWARD RABBITS."

Demane, sick and tired of the bullshit, nevertheless waded in.

Making twelve, he added four limbs to the brawl's previous eight. Though a man speaks only wisdom—

even shouts it—does the mudslide, avalanche, cyclone choose to heed? Next Demane tried to pry the stranger loose. Clinging like a fanatic to his relic, Messed Up committed both hands to retaining the prize.

"You motherfuckers must think Messed Up *care*." He clarified his position: "Messed Up DON'T care! Messed Up don't *give* a shit!"

Even the world's strongest man has a hard limit. This he cannot do: overcome another very strong man supercharged with hysteria, unless he *cuts loose*. In case of which, be ready to accept punctured lungs, a spine stove in, spleen ruptured, or neck snapped. Said otherwise, Demane's choice was to talk Messed Up down, or else kill him. No third option.

He'd never cut loose in his life, and was hardly going to do so tonight, against a brother. For a ridiculous eternity, then—while strangers jeered and the brothers put their loudest faith in Demane—the three men waddled side to side, back and forth: one bawling swears, one sense, one silently biting. Then a boy or woman screamed—it was Walead, in fact—splitting the crowd's hoarse noise with a treble axe.

The captain was come.

The heel of a bloody hand blew past Demane's shoulder, staunching the flow of Messed Up's raving upon impact. That clobbering strike knocked the colossus of the riot slack in Demane's arms, and loose from the stranger—who absconded. Quick as that first blow, another came just behind. Demane pivoted, taking the captain's fist on the hard meat of his shoulder, lest Messed Up's lolling head receive a lethal excess. *That* hurt. Both big men sagged toward the ground. With all the gentleness he could, Demane laid out Messed Up's deadweight. The brotherly part of the crowd surged inward.

"Damn it, Captain, he *down*!"

"Why you *hitting* him again? Dag!"

"Cain't you see the man out *cold*?"

Captain spun on them, his seeing eye wild. *Got whoop-ass to go around! Who else wants some?*

Not a brother did, and they swept—tidelike—out again. Demane got Messed Up turned on one side, the red flux of his nose wetting the cobbles, no longer drowning him.

"It's all right now, Isa." Demane caught the hem of Captain's robe above a sandaled foot. "I got him. Won't be no more trouble out of him or nobody. I mean it." He let go, and patted the instep.

At that touch strange sound and overheated odor bloomed into the night from the captain, recollections of some long-ago event. Demane caught his breath at the intensity. He smelled seabrine, waterlogged wood; he heard combers foaming, surf breaking. Trade winds blew in from the austral continent, full of spice and pollens unknown to him. And what *stench* was that ... the bloody ordure of a market butcheryard? The site of some big-game slaughter, buffalo or elephant? No; already attuned to the scent of Captain's blood, and Messed Up's, Demane recognized this vast spilled quantity as *human* blood ... several dozen men, gutted, all of whom had died within moments of one another. The corpses overcrowded some tightly enclosed space near the ocean ... rocking atop it: a ship. The captain stood tottering over him, and shed these remembered sensations so potently, Demane could have pointed to where each phantom body lay, eviscerated in the suffocating swelter. There was a scent-memory of the captain as well among those massed corpses, his unearthly blood leaking, the signature tattoo of his strong heart feeble and stuttering ... Then it broke, whether rapport or fugue, whatever that nightmare had been. Demane was again at the Station of Mother of Waters, fifteen hundred miles from any ocean. At the edge of the desert this warm night was cool— sweet indeed—beside that memory out of Hell.

Captain looked down at Demane, then all around. *Who are you? Where am I?* said these looks. The back-splash of other men's blood freckled his face, which was some stranger's, it was so pummeled and cut. His cyclopean left eye glared, his right one swollen up blind. The knuckles of his hands were raw gore, the flesh stripped in spots to glimpses of bone. By slow changes in stance and expression Demane marked the captain's return from wandering among ghosts and memories, to this night, these people. He stepped away from Demane's hand. He slumped to one side, swayed as though to fall and then, catching himself, painfully stood back upright.

Of course a doctor who was also lover would wish for nothing except to say, Let me help you. But more forthcoming than anything a man can ever say aloud— whether you may care for his wounds, whether you may watch over his sleep—is the silent testimony of his bearing and demeanor. For the body tells all to him who knows the language, and doesn't lie. The captain would sooner have leapt into the fiery lake atop Mt. Bittersmoke than accepted even so much as a shoulder to lean on.

Captain staggered off, one-leg-dragging, into darkness and glare. Brothers flushed from his way like pigeons from a loose dog.

Messed Up mumbled and stirred.

T-Jawn knelt beside Demane. "I should be only too happy to fuck right off again, if you are still wroth with me. But, please, Sorcerer, permettez-moi: shall I take feet or shoulders?"

"Salright." Demane lurched to a squat and then— making faces, all a-tremble—came to standing: hefting

Messed Up in his arms. "I got him."

"Mais, mon vieux! Are you *quite* sure . . . ?"

"Yeah, Jawny. Just get em out the way for me." De-mane nodded toward the brothers uselessly crowding in. And to that most useless pair:

"Xho, Walé!" Demane called. "Tell me where y'all staying at."

Nearby, in some travelers' barracks. The adobe hall was low-ceilinged, the doors narrow, and most of the brothers shared the biggest room in back. Men dropped onto their pallets, and into sleep within a breath or two. A few sat up whispering in the dark, rehearsing the night's events to one another. He laid Messed Up on the pallet nearest the window. Demane blinked to clear his eyes.

No longer bleeding, the nose was swollen tight as if to burst. He propped Messed Up's head on a rolled sheet, broached a jar of sterile water, and washed away caked blood. Flexing tiny muscles, praying under his breath, Demane began to nurse down a precious drop of ichor from his third eye. *Forgive me this venom. It is weak and will save a life, taking none. In* TSOA *they say, Let us hasten to the heat death, for its arrival is inevitable. Yet in TSIM we say, No; we shall keep on fixing the machine unto the last moment. So then account me TSIMtsoa, spinning on the Tower's right. Forgive me this venom . . .* Those brothers still awake gaped blindly toward this catechistic mutter.

The light too dim for their eyes, they started at the little sounds Demane made, taking from his bag and putting back.

He prayed, blinking, and then at last his tongue deliquesced. It split into tapered, coiling halves: the hot prehensile right, the cold secretory left—from which expressed a droplet viscid as quicksilver. Demane scooped up the mercurial drop in his venom sac, and faster than eyes rewet themselves with a blink, lashed half his tongue across a full yard, stroking its load precisely across the crushed bridge of Messed Up's nose. At once the black swelling went brown. Demane, blinking, allowed the vitriol a moment to anesthetize, to sink as deeply as bone. Then he pinched the nose's jumbled rubble back into order. His tongue sealed and shortened, trembling and achy. Estranged from his own emotion and fatigue, he cleaned wounds, sewing some. He kept having to blink to clear away his leaking tears. And why tears? Why *not*? This night had been long, trying, and widely various in its trials. And now that the last of the fires was all put out, he must not forget to grab by the neckscruff the rascals who set this blaze, and make them contemplate the smoky ruins.

"Xho and Walé, you two listen up." Demane began to pack up his *medicia*. "What happen is, sometimes qaïf can go bad, see, and [mycotoxic fungus] grow on it . . .

like a rot, you understand? That's why you don't smoke it. *Shouldn't.* Smoke some bad qaïf, and it [can induce choleric schizophrenia] . . . mess up your head for good. That's what *he* done a long time ago, what messed him up in the first place. Qaïf *poison*, very dangerous. It's [an insult to the homeostasis of body and mind]. You understand me?" Well, how can they, fool? You're speaking half in your own language!

Anxious to demonstrate rehabilitation, Xho Xho and Walead said, "We ain't smoking no more."

"Nope. Not again, uh uh."

"I don't even really *like* qaïf, never did. You, Walé?"

"*Hell* no—I *hate* that shit!"

There was a bit of back-and-forth over whether that one dude, or Messed Up, or indeed some other dude, had first thought it a good idea to do something so bad— "Myself, I was like, 'I don't think we *should*, though, y'all. I don't think it's *right.*'"—but certainly neither of *them*, the two boys concurring here, had been the original instigator.

Such eagerness to create space between present self and past sins obliges adults in the room to wonder whether callow youth has really wised up. "What if the fo-so had showed up?" Cumalo spoke harshly from the dark. "What if Captain had gone upside y'all peanut heads hard as he did Messed Up?"

"He *has* before."

"Yup! Cause, remember that time? I couldn't see straight for *days* . . ."

The noise of frustration Demane made turned to a huge yawn. His burning eyes, all at once, would hardly stay open.

T-Jawn groped for Demane's shoulder. "You sound all done in, Sorcerer. Vous pouvez partir, and take your rest. Messrs. Xho Xho and Walead shall retire for the evening, while Cumalo and I keep our eyes on things. I daresay no further mischief can be forthcoming from our sleeper— not tonight, non?"

So Demane left.

There was to be, after all, no rendezvous, laid up to- gether under palm tree fronds on the banks of Mother of Waters. That hope had always been a mirage, though anticipation of it had carried Demane through all the weeks of the desert crossing. Now he'd find some spot in the open air to sleep beside the lake. But not quite yet: a night so evil required exorcizing before sleep. Wise words, or even the company of wisdom though nothing was said, would be enough. Along empty alleys, Demane returned to the piazza. The throngs there had become stragglers, and the awful fluorescence of the greatorch banked down to a sulfurous glow. And yes: Faedou and his jar even now sat against the wall. Demane took seat beside his elder brother. Content to say nothing, they watched the remnants of the night revels.

A lone drummer beat his jimbay with closed eyes, inspiring the feet of the last score dancers. Two of the caravan's merchants, Qabr and Iuliano, slowstepped tiredly and in synch among those final revolving few. The two men possessed the same fine manners, eloquent hands, and trim small size: alike as twins, though obviously *not* kin—the one being pale and sharp-featured; the other dark, full of mouth and nose. What a blessing, what wonderful good luck, Demane thought, to make this long crossing with such a friend to share the travails. Never did you see those two apart! One night years ago perhaps they'd twirled through the piazza's crowd and bumped into each other for the first time. And now, in memory of that first night perhaps it was their habit to dance away another whenever passing through town—

"*Tch.*" Faedou sucked his teeth, scowling. "It ain't right." He nodded toward the merchants dancing. "You know them two be smoking, right?"

Demane shook his head. "No, Faedou, not those two." Men of such quality would never touch qaïf, and he said so.

"No, man." With thumb upright, Faedou pursed his lips and crudely mimed the act he meant. "You know— 'unnatural connections.'" He turned his head aside and spat. "*Faggits.*"

"Slate," Demane said finally (for you need to be braced when such a roundhouse comes in, or else it knocks the breath right out of you). He clapped hands down against his knees. "Bout time for me to go lay down." He stood and while turning away tapped Faedou's shoulder. "Don't be out here all night, old man."

Demane made his way to the lakeshore. The moon had set. Passing the canvas slums, his steps in the gravel brought some lady to a tent's open flaps. She was about the age of his own mother. From within, he heard her pickney sleeping, a child's slow, even breaths. The matron could have made out his silhouette, nothing more, in this dim starlight; still, she called to him, "Sex you, poppy?" as he went by.

By Mother of Waters he unfolded a buffalo hide onto the sands, and stretched out. The lake breathed coolly over his skin. The sand beneath his groundsheet leached heat up into his body. An unbroken field of stars, the sky glittered without a single spot wholly dark. His blood whispered to him of the first Home, *there*, a flickering as yellow as firelight, no brighter than ten billion other stars. Demane might still have people up there. Cousins.

And with her to marshal us, we then were able to bind the wild depths of time and space, as well as those [anachronisms] and [extradimensionalities] that had come ravening therefrom. We asked, *How shall we call you,* and she answered, *Howsoever; for my name has no acoustics but is rather [scent-pheromone-fragrance] and you lack the faculty to [utter] it.* So we named her Preema because she was first in power. Preema, before taking leave of us, said *let one of you magi forsake your Enclave and assume dominion over that place. For the Wild Depths cannot remain so but must needs be mastered.* Before any could obey her, we were beset by the dragons that burnt Daluz, and iron dogs which came out of the eastern bush; there was also war with Hell, with the so-called Children of the Lie; and earthquake and plague and famine racked our friend and neighbor, Great Olorum: so that for all of a generation, and much of the next, the talents of the magi were sore-tried. By the time of the Respite, no magi living knew how to effect that mastery which Preema had enjoined; but anyway the Road was still holding safe three centuries after laying the greatwork, then as now.

from [ancestral eidetic memory] of the magi
of the Ashëan Enclave

Fifth of Seven

Hey, I gave you the choice, didn't I? Sit jawing or make love. And you didn't choose "talk," so don't try to change it up now.

Southbound from Mother of Waters, eldest brother rode his burro between the two youngest, and told them tales—filling up the green brakes and jungle the caravan approached with a tribe of rapacious cannibals.

No. Suresh paid me no mind; I told you that he wouldn't.

The name of this cannibal tribe was supposed to be *"sharken"*: so called because they had mouths full of crooked sawteeth in double rows, like the pale maneaters that preyed upon fishermen and pearl divers on the northern coasts; called *sharken* too, for that way of theirs, lurking invisibly in the shadows: until such moment as they brought down swift, terrible death upon the unawares.

You have to understand, man. They sank whole fortunes into this caravan, Suresh and the merchants. The Great Father, God, couldn't make them turn back or aside now. We'll just have to keep an eye out, you and me.

These folk—extraordinarily plump and well fed, fanged and wholly merciless—refused all meats except for tender cuts flayed off the shanks of men—and boys, especially—who set unwary feet off-Road while traveling through the Wildeeps.

Mmm … but no more, D. I'm serious now. That's enough. Are you listening? Are you going to let me go? I need to get down to the emburdening. And you need to go roust the brothers out of bed, make sure everybody gets over to Suresh's on time. And unless I say so, D.: no brother steps off-Road, nobody. You tell them.

He wanted only to savor this mood, pure joy. Demane dropped a word to the wise, but decided that somebody else, just this once, could go about marshaling the scrappy forces of good sense, those few and sore-beset, against the nigh-invincible armies of foolish hard-headedness. Anyway, it was often true that fear best motivated fools; in which case no one was better suited than Faedou, so deft with a scary story, for persuading Xho Xho and Walead to keep to the straight course. That old man could have you jumping at the knock of your own heart!

"Just thought you two might like a little heads up," said Faedou. "Cause those sharken will fry your ass up with some peppers and onions in a *heartbeat*. Watch out, is all I'm really saying here."

Xho Xho and Walead doubted.

This one said, "You *know* you lying, Faedou!"

And that one: "Ain't no cannibals in the Wildeeps!"

"Well." Faedou wearily shook his head. "It's on you, then." There was very much a feeling he'd done all any man could: some folks were just doomed. *Nothing* could save them. "Go on off-Road into them woods if you want to, I guess." The very cadences of his voice evoked the scene: two young brothers joking, acting a fool, the leaf shadows, some twig breaks, one or the other would whisper (his last words) *Man, did you just hear that? What was that?* then nothing but screams, blood splattering, limbs in flight asunder from torsos. Both our young heroes ripped horribly to bits. As if to get it right for the eulogy, Faedou asked, "Wha'chall got, sixteen, seventeen years? Not a long life. *Sad* is what it is. But, yeah, I known some brothers to go that young. Always a damn shame, though."

Walead sucked his teeth. Xho Xho drew a deep breath, trying to make his caved chest seem barrel. "I ain't *never* scared!" And yet didn't these two, of all the brothers and merchants, keep most cautiously to the Road? During the hailstorm, Walead and Xho Xho even took a savage beating rather than run for shelter with the rest. The boys pissed from the dirt into the green, fell to the rear of the baggage train for squats right there center-

Road, before running to catch up with the caravan's stragglers.

Aunty was sister neither to his mother nor father, but seven times the great-grandmother of the former, and five times the latter. She'd neglected to die in the way of other people, and came back through the green hills once or twice each generation. When Demane was six years old, Aunty came again and word went around that nobody younger than thirty should fail to visit her next full moon morning. She meant to teach some likely youth or child to work miracles.

"Now, I want you to *stay* your little backside right here in the house." Demane's mother held his chin firmly, keeping his gaze fixed to hers. "Do you hear me talking, little boy?"

"Yes, ma'am." What he couldn't understand was why his younger brother and older sister—in fact, *the entire world*—got to go to Aunty's gathering. Everyone except for him. "But I want to come too!"

Whenever Mama took a hard line, sometimes it worked to appeal to Papa. This time, however: "You do what your mama said, Mountain Bear." His parents looked at each other, an exchange full of tacit secrets.

They shed a strange and particular frequency of fear-scent—as before, when Demane used to sniff the air and offer careless remarks concerning someone's mood, or recent whereabouts. But he knew better now, and never did that anymore, *ever*, so there was no justice in these deserts, this punishment. The family left. He stayed.

Some are hellions, and some children a comfort to their parents; some, take your eyes off them for an instant, and they're already into every sort of mischief. Until that day, Demane had always belonged to that rare few to whom you might speak one gentle word and then trust to obey. But after the family had gone, he waited a while in terror and excitement—then he too donned his wickleaf cloak, and ran out into the rainy forest, toward the big gathering-house.

The caravan left the Station much later than planned, not at crack of dawn but nigh unto noon; still, they rode without haste down toward the Wildeeps. It often happens that, when the revels of a night have passed, and the sun sits on high again, a long day follows where nothing much gets done, or only half-assed and very slowly. For the suffering is widespread and horrendous as men repent what they did and shouldn't have the night before.

Speaking to the general sentiment, Barkeem said, "That Demon will fuck you up, mayne. I'm hungover as shit."

"Somebody kept passing me the jar, though," said another brother riding, squinty eyed, at one side. "Do any of y'allses head feel like it's gon' bust?"

Yeah, said a majority.

"We had all better partaken, I warrant, of that potion which does allow the Sorcerer to smile so," said T-Jawn; "yea, though the sun beats down, and my head cracks apart. For *there* rides a man qui ne sait rien de notre douleur!"

"He *do* look kinda happy, though, don't he?"

"Damn, Sorcerer; all your teeth showing! What you got to grin about?"

"For real, my dude—I need a sip of whatever *you* had!"

Demane couldn't dim the grin, nor even get his lips covering his teeth. "Just a beautiful day out here, is all. Won't y'all let young Demane be glad for once?"

"*Tch.* Cain't nobody tell me that brother didn't get him a piece last night. Ain't nothing but some reeeeeeeally good ass gon' have a man smiling like *that.*"

"Teef, don't start up. You know the Sorcerer ain't been up in them damn tents carrying on. It's true love or nothing for him. Right, Sorcerer? "

"That's right, Kazza. Me and the Station just didn't get along too good. So it feel nice to be on road again."

The afternoon reddened and evening came on and still Demane felt in remarkable charity with the world. Slow thunderheads bore down on them. No: as the caravan drew nearer the Crossings they saw it was the towering clouds that stayed put, while their own progress southward overtook the stationary storm.

Men and their burros straggled out along the Crossings' pebbled north shore. Oldtimers said nothing should have been easier than to look across the broad shallows and spot the Road, a wide black gap in the jungle's green wall. But fog had rolled east to west across the south bank as far as eyes could see, and hard rain was falling over the Wildeeps, and only over there. The skies above the caravan were clear.

"See, this what they *need* to do," said Michelo. "Stack up some stones over here on *this* side—see what I'm saying—to mark where the Road is at over *there*."

"Yeah!" Wilfredo said. "Then you could find that shit, no matter if it was all foggy over the Wildeeps."

"No," said Faedou. "Y'all don't get it. That wouldn't work."

"Why not, pray?" said T-Jawn. "Some signpost—a waymark—raised here on the north shore, just across from the Road là-bas: that strikes me a *fine* idea, Faedou."

"Problem is," said the old man, "it would be 'way-marks' all up and down the Crossings. The Road don't keep to just one spot. Moves around."

Across unspeakably vast vacancies, the nearest star blew toward the earth a wind of poisonous fire, which passed harmlessly through the sphere's upper firmament, never catastrophically across the living surface, thanks to a field surrounding the earth, which fixed the location of all things on the planet by means of subtle pressure-lines palpable to birds, and other sensitive beings. Thanks, of course, to that undimmable brightness in the sky above the Road, Demane could see precisely where it began; but he knew moreover that the Road had shifted in relation to the northbank, nearly three miles eastward from yesterday's latitude. He wasn't sure it was wise to admit any of this knowledge.

He urged his burro nearer the riverbank. Six or seven merchants were there wrangling with Master Suresh over what was to be done. Astride his own burro, the caravan-master peered at the farshore with a hand at his brow, as if a brave pose might help him see through lashing rain and dense fog. Gathered about and querulously howling at him was that quarter of the merchants most difficult to please. The sense of the mob seemed to be that it was too early to call halt for the day; certainly not before reaching the first well on the Road. There was the feeling too that the rain and fog, that the Road should be hidden from view, represented an outrageous dereliction of Suresh's responsibilities as caravanmaster.

The remainder of merchants, and the brothers, all rested, letting their burros graze or drink. Most lay sacked out in the grass, a hood or sleeve drawn over their eyes, while awaiting some decision to come down. Demane examined the caravan for any other who showed signs of being able to see the sky beacon that marked the Road.

Oh, and whence this high, fine mood of his? Demane had retreated at dawn to a leafy bower in the thickets surrounding Mother of Waters, for the sun rose too bright and timely for further sleep on the sands. But neither had those deep shadows been a site for sleep: he'd just stretched out, just closed his eyes, when the last man expected had come crawling under the briars to him. For such a long time Demane had felt parched and colorless as the landscape through which the caravan had come wending down from Mother of Waters. And how did he feel now, as it got on for dusk, at the threshold of the Wildeeps? Well. Even as this cracked gray earth would revive under the softest downpour, there had fallen on Demane, as it were, a sweet and drenching rain. And just as this dust and these rocks, rained-upon, might sheen over with fresh verdancy, so was Demane turning a toothy grin onto everyone—glad in his heart!—body satisfied, his every thought a hopeful one. Picture the badlands blooming with many-colored wildflowers: some snow-white as eyes rolled back in ecstasy, others the incarnadine of wet lips slack and ajar in desire's surcease; and little blossoms, springing up among the new grass, mauve as a lover's bruised flanks, your hands *so* gently steadying his half of the act up and down in place, on your lap. And where's he, now? There! Captain stood in the water, the reins of his burro in hand, while the hard current creamed about his ankles and its hooves. He stared cross-river and upwards, at that folded lightning bolt in the sky, shining through rain and fog, marking the Road.

Last night's injuries from the Fighthouse could have been healing a fortnight rather than only one, by the looks. At dawn, there'd been nothing halt in Captain's movements, no wincing wherever touched. Those torn knuckles had already grown thick dry scab. Demane himself was quick to heal from wounds, but hardly like this, not overnight. Now, at the day's second twilight, about to cross over into the Wildeeps, even the scabs on Captain's hands had fallen away, and the skin of his knuckles showed raw and pale, not yet tawnied to the proper brownish gold. His bruises, not livid: faded; and the last remnant wound, his left eye, only a little puffy, but fully open, its sclera white and clear.

Startled, Captain spun about—as happened often when anyone's regard tarried too long on him. He and Demane spoke then, entirely in nods and glances, a conversation that might be rendered thus:

You see that there?

Sure do.

What should we do?

My man, YOU the captain.

Well, I can't speak in front of all those merchants. Go and tell Master Suresh for me where we should cross for the Road. . . . Please?

Come on now, I'm just another one of the brothers! You know it's not right making me talk to the caravanmaster!

All right, all right. I'll go too and support what you say, but you speak for me. Let's go.

Are you ready to admit yet, chump—that you're the softest touch there is? Demane sighed. Dismounting he gave his reins to the brother beside him. Then, walking over to Master Suresh amidst the fractious merchants, he felt his stomach sour. However well Demane understood Merqerim, he spoke that dialect poorly. In a bad mood, the caravanmaster liked to mock a foreigner nastily, pretending not to understand a bad accent. It was a bit rough on the feelings, to tell the truth. Demane tried to work up a few short phrases in his head. But you were forever changing the ending-sound of words in Merqer-im, which had to go in a very precise order, which was al-so ever-changing . . . About to turn and say, *no, look, wait,* the objection was checked with a touch. The captain lay a hand between Demane's shoulder blades, and sliding that hand to the small of his back, top of his ass, steered Demane through the press of merchants. A friend's touch—a touch that meant nothing, one that didn't count—would have been flat and firm, not there and gone, so maddeningly light. *Chump!*

"Master Suresh, the Road, she," (he, it? shoot! which one?) "is right there. I see she." (No, *her,* shouldn't it be? Yes, it should.)

"What? Are you claiming to know where the Road is?" Peering down, Master Suresh l'Merqerim blinked and bugged his eyes, as if he'd never seen Demane before: this unasked for barbarian in his state of folkloric un-dress, quite an outlandish interloper, among the garbed and sober colloquies of civilization. "Now I forget: which one would you be? *Odell,* is it—or is your name *Birthday Suit?*" Master Suresh enjoyed the pretence that his guardsmen, none of them, were to be told from one an-other, any more than a perfect stranger from his identical twin. No brother was exempt from this indignity except the captain, who (slick as a snake) had disappeared some few steps back.

The merchant Iuliano said, "Oh, Suresh, what can you be playing at? This strapping fellow could *never* be mistaken for another! He is the guardsman the rest of them call 'the Sorcerer.'" Iuliano's regard was warm—a bit chilly, though, that of his man Qabr, riding beside him.

"I, Demane, yes. And the Road is there." Demane pointed crossriver upstream. "Right there. I sure. I *am* sure." Aback their burros, the high-toned crowd all turned to look where Demane pointed. Utterly featureless to their eyes, that foggy bank billowed high as heaven, the color of smoke and ash. They looked back at him; but before the clamor of disbelief could break out, the captain shoved forward. He draped a certifying arm across Demane's shoulders and said, "It's true," his voice as little beautiful, as much gruff* as he could make it. Demane forgave the little disappearing act and fell in love all over again, or more so. Whichever. Both.

The impending uproar dispersed into murmurs.

"You know as well as I, Captain, what doom befalls that caravan which strays off the safe path. If we cross to

---

* Who minds, on the season's very best day, the briars on the bushes of the rosegarden? No one, Captain. And what man given a treat—who's gone without, who has a sweet tooth—even notices the bits of comb in your honey? No man, Captain.

the far bank and attempt to wander the perilous wood hoping to chance upon the Road, all our lives may be forfeit. Are you sure then, Captain Isa, we can follow this, this *sorcerous* fellow?"

The captain nodded. Suresh stood in his stirrups and bellowed: "FORM UP."

She showed her other face to him. "You're not scared, are you?"

"No, Aunty." Demane looked up; and he'd thought her tall *before*! "Let me see your teeth again."

She grinned: a maw full of ivory spikes. When she stretched out both arms, unfurling veiny thinskinned wings, Demane laughed and jumped up and down. "Fly! Go up in the air with them!"

"Not by day, child." She put down her arms. "Maybe I'll take you up after dark. If your cousins see something just *small* and wonderful, they're ready to scream and cover their eyes. Can you imagine if they saw me looking this way, flying around?"

"I want to change too! Teach me *that*."

"Ah, Demane, we'll just have to see, now, won't we? There's only a spot of old blood left in you, but it *is* possible. You've got the blood-grace stronger than just about anybody I've seen these last couple generations."

Every talon on her massive hands looked as bladed and sharp as his mother's gutting knife. Demane tested with a fingertip.

"*Careful*, boy!"

"Ouch."

———

They forded and crossed the wall of fog. Beyond it, a muggy mist crept along the ground at knee height, and broken cloudcover spat single fat drops, not hard rain. Nothing grew from the black dirt of the Road, which was wide enough for ten to ride abreast. The jungle at either side wasn't continuous trees but intermittent stands, all overgrown with creepers, moss, and ferns. Between one copse and the next grew tracts of brakes and elephant grass. The greatwork on the Road dimmed Demane's senses such that, eerily, he could plumb the steamy green landscape with hardly more than human clarity, his scent and taste and hearing so vague and weak that—

"Hey, Sorcerer. You can *ride* that burro, you know. Why you down there walking in the dirt?"

Because he could take the Road's measure only by touch, through his bare feet. And what had he learned of the Road? "I'm too big," Demane said, patting at his burro. "Gotta give the poor guy a break every now and then."

"They small, but just as strong as camels," Faedou said. "Son, it ain't hurting him none for you to ride."

"Naw, naw. *I'll* tell you why he walking," Xho Xho said. "Sorcerer wanna be hard like the captain. *That's* why!"

Walead said, "Yup, yup," and even Faedou smiled, for there was a whiff of the plausible about that explanation. To keep his body stropped to a razor's-edge condition, Captain rarely rode; he jogged at the forefront of the caravan for most of every day. For such unflinching commitment to doing everything the hardest way possible, the brothers all thought him a bit mad; Demane too.

"Was I *really* trying to be hard like Captain," Demane said, "I'd haveta snatch you sideways for talking smart, Xho."

Walead cackled, and Faedou said, "Sorcerer got you right there, young brother!"

The butt of his spear thumped against the earth. Demane understood little about the greatwork laid over the Road—except that it was unimaginably powerful, and its warding virtue undiminished. But a jukiere wasn't native to the Wildeeps, and so as free to wander from woods to Road as Demane himself.

———————

"I'm going to leave the bag here with you." Aunty handed it to him. "It's better to have it out in the world, in good hands. And you're the best one of mine I've seen come along since the last time I rested. Now, stop that, Mountain Bear! Cut out all that crying right now, and I *mean* it. You start up, you'll get me going too. I told you I was old, boy. Some of these hills aren't old as me. Anyway, I'm not necessarily passing on. Just, when I lay me down this time, I'm going to have a good *long* sleep. Might be I don't wake up again."

———————

Not long past first light on the second day, the pale and cloudy morning turned lilac, and then murkier still. At intervals livid fire brightened the skies, with thunder cracking hard by. A strange rain began to fall: stinging, gritty, almost like spatters of scalding water.

"What *is* this shit?" Teef held out a cupped hand trying to catch the hard, hot water.

Or no, not hot at all—the downpour was so *cold*, it seemed to burn.

"I know," Cumalo exclaimed. "I saw this up in the Titans once, crossing the mountains. It's called *snow*."

A merchant screamed then, and right thereafter so did everyone else. The burros brayed and fought on their leads. From above and all sides, pebbles and goodsized stones pelted the caravan savagely.

"No," Demane said, "it's hail!" Right here, the worlds on and off this stretch of Road happened to be aligned in time and place. So, it might be safer for them to . . . Captain looked at Demane and nodded sharply. The Sorcerer shouted, "Get under the trees!"

The caravan abandoned the Road. Monkeys shrieked and gibbered overhead in the canopy. Torrents of ice thrashed the leaf cover, making a terrific noise, the foliage drifting thickly down in green tatters and rags.

Several brothers sheltered beneath the same huge tree as Demane. "Why don't you pull something outta that bag for these fucken sky-rocks?" Teef said. "*Do* something, Sorcerer!"

He was just talking smart, but Demane answered anyway. "Aunty never taught me anything for this."

"Huh?"

He'd spoken his mothertongue, but Demane didn't repeat himself, only shook his head.

They weathered the hailstorm well enough under the trees. Few stones reached them under the canopy, and those hit harmlessly, all force lost passing through the density of leaves and limbs.

The freak storm quickly passed, the clouds lifting and whitening. There was afterwards a tedious business of accounting for things and persons, recapturing the scattered burros, two of which lay dead, tongues lolling beside ice-chunks of skull-crushing size. Walead and Xho Xho had never left the open Road. Hail had pummeled them bloody. Walead was hysterical with terror and pain, Xho Xho stunned and clingy. Demane cleaned their cuts, having to sew and bandage the worst. In the manner that comforts, he fussed over them; but Walead was inconsolable. At last Demane resorted to a drop of poppy philter under the boy's tongue.

A merchant had gone missing. Naturally no one had seen or heard anything. The friend of Iuliano, Qabr, came and knelt beside Demane. "When your call rang out to take shelter beneath the trees, I fled without thinking to one side of the Road, Iuly to the other." Helplessly his suave hand gestured east, then west. "Everyone swears to know nothing. But *you*, Mr. Sorcerer, I have heard them say, are the best tracksman and hunter among us. Will you not have a look about?" The merchant Qabr caught one of Demane's hands in his, and pressed beseechingly. What to say but yes, of course?

He made to stand; Xho Xho grabbed at him. "Hey, little man, hey there," Cumalo said, prying loose the fingers, nodding *Go* to Demane. "Check this out! Sorcerer ain't the only one, you know. I got tricks too." Cumalo took out his bone dice.

He went to the captain, who then spoke to Master Suresh: the caravan was told to make ready for travel, and then to wait. Captain and Demane, one on either side, worked the grounds with slow steps for longer than the muster could patiently abide. Guardsmen began to joke and laugh. Merchants complained bitterly to Master Suresh of time wasted, daylight lost. The forest thereabouts was such a trampled mess and profusion of scents and sign, blurred beneath rain and melting hail, Demane couldn't hope for pugmarks. And he found none, nor any splashed blood, either (and the merchant Iuliano was so slight, so small-boned, that a jukiere might have lifted the man off the ground and carried him away, instead of dragging the body...), but at length he stopped short and called, "Captain!" The crowd on the Road fell silent, staring.

Demane pointed without explanation into the shadows where a dense growth of leaning canebrake half-hid clods of dung.

Master Suresh l'Merqerim rushed to them. "What have you found? Is that lion scat? It looks fresh!" The man spun about wildly, as if to spot the crouching predator before it sprang. But the thick grass surrounding them might have covered a whole pride, and the nearby copse, elephants. "Has a lion taken him?"

The merchant Qabr wafted nearer, listening, both arms crossed before him, either hand draping the opposite shoulder.

The captain squatted down. With a woody length of cane, he poked apart the moist rubble, and with the stick's point, nudged forth a mudcaked bit of wool. Sharply he looked upwards. Demane, who leaned over him, had grunted.

"You're sure?" the captain sang *leggiero.*

"Ain't a doubt in my mind."

"What?" Master Suresh l'Merqerim looked back and forth between them. "I see nothing here but a shitty piece of fur. What does this signify?"

The captain, sotto voce to Demane: "Many beasts have dark fur. A boar, perhaps—?"

"Baby, come on." Demane sucked his teeth. "You see them curls too tight. How you gon' tell me they come off some pig?"

"All right"—the captain's song grim now—"all right." He stood.

"Yes? He said what? *Tell* me, Captain Isa! What is the meaning of all that bushman rabble-babble?"

Impatiently, Captain sang a long line. "Demane understands your every word perfectly, Master Suresh l'Merqerim."

"And *what*? I insist that you—!"

"It was no lion dropped this dung, Master Suresh. And that is not fur, but a piece from a man's scalp. The jook-toothed tiger has eaten someone before."

He was singing past the caravanmaster, to Qabr. Captain sang in a minor key, inflected with blue notes. At once Qabr grasped the vanity of hope. He made a northern man's sound of terrible pain: a scream swallowed, choked upon. Then the small man opened his mouth wide and wailed.

Neither Demane nor the captain found any other sign.

Ashé's children wish us well,

but never trust them, born of Hell.

TsimTsoa's by far the best,

for weal and woe, than all the rest!

> **from** "Tower Song," chanted for skip-stone
>
> games in Great Olorum

Sixth of Seven

Master Suresh required them to pick up the pace. One stop, once a day, at the midday well; nor would they linger there. The caravan would press on as near full dark as possible. He wanted them across the Wildeeps in four nights, though the customary number was six.

Things shook out otherwise.

The skies slowly dimmed, an overcast louring, black and heavy. As this premature night fell, the malevolence of the flanking forests seemed to close in upon them. By late afternoon the feeble daylight had nearly died. From the blustery dark above, rain fell softly on them: *very* cold. The tropical evening waxed ever chillier, the breeze freshening from moment to moment, until it cut raw and harsh. Men saw their breath—many for the first time. Merchants and brothers who had them pulled out second and third robes and every blanket and scrap of cloth they owned, the caravan swaddling itself up. Some dismounted to trot alongside their burros, warming themselves with exertion. Demane slipped lightly into trance.

"Ain't you cold like that, Sorcerer?"

"Yeah, I'm freezing my *ass off* just looking at you!"

"Si no tieneh con qué abrigarte, take my blanket, Sorcerer. Here."

"I'm straight, Willy," said Demane. "You keep it." The fine drizzle, no sooner alighting, dried from Demane's skin, and ghostly vapor wished about him. "I got my inside-fires burning high." He reached and patted the cheek of each brother in turn: Wilfredo, Teef, Barkeem.

"You burning up hot!" Wilfredo grabbed Demane's hand tight, as if to squeeze some heat into his own numb fingers. "¿Cómo lo haceh? Teach me!"

"All right. But answer me this: Will you sit still half the day, every day, for the next five years?"

"¡*Coño!* The trick take so long to learn?"

"Could be longer," Demane said. "Some people, they thoughts won't settle down, and just keep jumping around like monkeys..."

He didn't tell them that this winter, small and local, was stalking them across the Wildeeps. Just off-Road, a few steps away, it was steamy and hot beneath the trees, the drizzle falling blood-warm. The evening, there, was orange and bright, not clouded and dark as the last watch before dawn. This weather was more jukiere mischief. Well before sundown, daylight had nearly expired, and so Master Suresh had to call halt far earlier than he'd wished. Few had tents, or any recourse but to lie down in the mud, rained upon, wrapped in wet and sour-smelling blankets.

In such bedraggled straits Xho Xho sat, embraced by his own thin arms. The brown-blotched white bandages swathing his gashed scalp and forehead were wet through with rainwater. "Cain't you do something, Sorcerer?" The boy spoke through rattling teeth. "Pleeeeease?"

"Aw, Xho." Demane sat too; sharing out the hot fruits of an accelerated metabolism, he put his arm around the boy. "You don't really think I could just open my bag, and the sky would clear up, do you?"

Aunty had very rarely scrupled to work the weather, saying that far too easily you might misalign patterns of drought and flood the whole sphere over; he'd one time, however, seen her break a full-blown cyclone into mere brisk wind and rain. So no doubt *she* could have waved away this conjured inclemency, but such feats were well beyond him.

"*Something*, Sorcerer. Anything." Xho Xho huddled under the heat of Demane's arm. "You sure it ain't *nothing* you can do?"

Demane thought, *Well . . .* and a whiff of his hesitant consideration must have communicated itself to the boy, for he threw off Demane's arm and seized his hand in supplication. *Would you be healed? Show faith!* quoth the Patriarch in verses of Holy Recitature, speaking unto a mendicant leper. And with belief and fervor and pleas quite like that sick man's, Xho Xho begged Demane.

"You *can* do something, Sorcerer! You got to, man: we dying out here!" Well, nobody was dying; but few in the caravan had ever known such bitter chill, and no one had come prepared for it.

"All right, all right." Demane shook free of the boy, fending off his histrionics. "Turn down some, little brother. I'll make a couple big fires."

"Never do I doubt you, mind," said T-Jawn, from the depths of his cowl. "Mais je voudrais remarquer que, even were these rains to cease, Sorcerer, *where* in all this Godforsaken show could we turn up dry wood?" T-Jawn waved broadly, a gesture encompassing the muddy Road, and the trees' plentiful deadfall strewn all over it. "Such as this will not burn."

"Even water burn, hot enough," Demane replied, and so he looked to Captain, and was given the nod. Brothers had gathered round about, for such had become the tendency when a problem was set before Demane. He drew the sort of deep, deep breath particular to the adept who means to dip into the perilous end of his knowledge. Slowly he let the breath out. "Don't even like *fooling* with this stuff, really," Demane said to them. "And, brothers, y'all listen to me. These fires could go all night, or might burn just *half* the night, all right? But let's start piling some wood up-Road a ways, not right here by the burros. Don't worry about tinder. All I need is sticks and big wood. Enough for two big fires, so everybody—merchants, too—could get warm."

They got to it.

Whoever is not master of all that arises, in every instant, was never master at all: Suresh l'Merqerim shot out from among the merchants, intent upon putting down what looked to be a mad uprising. The captain intercepted him, and lullabyishly sang down Suresh's obscenities and shouts. While the caravanmaster stood by, scowling and watching brothers gather the wood, Captain went back to helping disburden the burros for the night.

"Mostly *green* stuff," Walead said bitterly of the storm-fallen branches. "And *wet*." He and Xho Xho stripped the leaves from a heavy bough, and together dragged it to Demane; who stomped halfway down its length and, with a heave and grunt, broke the thick limb in twain.

Twice, Cumalo put down a crosshatched base of logs, and propped up the stick-towers to make two bonfires.

The sons and nephews traveling with the merchants were made to work like dogs. When the burros had all been unloaded and hobbled, given water from the well, and their buckets filled with fodder, the boys' uncles and fathers sent them to join the brothers' labors. Neither merchant nor boy asked how these heaping stacks of wood, drenched from the day's steady rain, would be set ablaze. Except by way of Master Suresh, the merchant elite never addressed their brotherly help. That was the way of things.

In the midst of all this activity Faedou stood looking like the very next man upon whom Death must call. Leaning tripod on his spear, and doddering from agony and chill, he could no longer be mistaken for his own son; more likely for his own grandfather, though a score years in the grave. Faedou's deep glossy color had gone ashen. Despite the cold, he stank of feverish sweat. And even stifled by the greatwork on the Road, Demane's nose knew well the nature of that sweetish rot wafting from the wound beneath his brother's robe. Demane went to him, tried to speak to him; but Faedou would not leave off his litany of prayers. Peevishly he shook his head, and as before, slapped away all offers of help.

The brothers called for Demane to bring the sorcery. The wood awaited, the two towers assembled, and so he had to leave Faedou's side.

Conical and about man-height, the pyres stood at center-Road, one ten long strides from the other.

Now, I'm warning you, Mountain Bear: they're not to be trifled with. The wisest thing would be to let them alone forever. I inherited these, and never touched them myself. So you want to think twice, and go ahead and think another time, before you call yourself trying to make use of them. I hope you're listening; I really do. Up and kill yourself, or somebody else, or burn down a whole town justlikethat. Aunty had given him many precautions, and Demane, crouched beside the first tower, needed a long moment to review them all. At his back, the muttersome pipe and rumble of men and boys.

"It's cold, the wood soaking wet," Walead complained. "I'm *tired*. It's raining on my Goddamn head. I don't see what we had to get all that wood for. How this gon' work? It *ain't* gon' work!"

"Yo, nigga! *Shut up* with that shit, will you?" said Xho Xho, though. "Sorcerer said he could, he CAN."

"Dang! You ain't got to get all mad, I'm just *saying . . .*"

His hand, his whole arm, in the depths of the bag, Demane felt through the straw cushioning a solid chest. He found a globe of sealed clay. He thought at first he'd misremembered there being two, and then his tentative fingers brushed the shape of the second. He shifted aside one of the upright logs, and tenderly set a sphere atop the interior base of stacked sticks and branches. Daylight was fast failing. He of course could see fine, but that only made it harder to judge a practical distance for other eyes. Far enough away for safety, yet close enough to make out this gap in the logs.

Not a single one of the caravan's twelve dozen looked

anywhere but at Demane's obscure antics. Boys shivered in the bite of sleety wind. Men blew onto curled fingers, stamping to get feeling back into bare sandaled feet. Demane called to the crowd, "Michelo!" and that brother came forth: he was the dead shot among them. Michelo could knock a bird from flight, or kill a bolting rabbit, with one thrown stone. "You see where it's a black hole in them sticks?"

Michelo leaned and squinted. " . . . think so."

Demane dropped a pebble into his hands.

Michelo's first throw struck a log, deflecting off into the shadows of the forest. Master Suresh l'Merqerim had seen enough. "Perhaps it's slops, not brains, in your skulls! Or is it rather piss and night soil?" Shouting, he came forward. "Can you not see, you simple no-school idjits, that the wood is wet? That God is pissing down rain?"

Michelo's second throw went true.

Luminous blue and yellow splashed from the clay sphere. Liquid-fire splattered within the bundled sticks and stacked logs; they caught, the wet wood combusting eagerly. Dark and dead one moment, the pyre was toweringly ablaze the next. Men exclaimed at the roar and sudden brilliance. Demane had made the crowd stand far back, but faint warmth washed them even there, and he had to shout down a general rush forward into luxurious heat. There was still the second pyre to be lit.

A single gobbet of bright jelly had splashed out of the wood tower, and glowed amidst the puddles of the Road. Undimmed by rain, like some imp from the fire-fields of Sol, it danced in the mud. Demane conjured a jar from his bag and with a single spilled drop quenched this molten errancy. He and Michelo kindled the other pyre.

The merchant Qabr refused to sleep fireside with the rest of the caravan; not for this evening, no. Too many eyes on him, the others all murmuring, and with Dom Iu-liano's . . . *absence*, it was all rather too much, just now. Sincere thanks, however, for the concern, very kind—*too* kind. Demane spoke of the safety in numbers, of the dangers to the outlier who wanders from the herd; but with poignant little gestures and appalled stares, the merchant inspired in Demane such a feeling of brutish presumption that his tongue tripped over these warnings. "Bay, would you talk to him? See what you could do?" But neither could the captain's most suasive song convince. Qabr sent back his nephews—one pale, one dark—to sleep among the crowds about the bonfires, after the boys had pitched the two-man tent in the darkness up-Road from the caravan proper. He went into the tent alone.

Captain quartered the night, as always. No brother was to stand still or sit while on watch. Five would walk up and down with their spears at all times. On nights past the captain himself had often watched three full quarters, and slept only when Demane—"*You*, nobody else"—was awake and on watch. It seemed he meant to do the same tonight. Captain stalked restlessly, with the camp, the Road, and Wildeeps at either side, all under his fierce regard. Never did you see such an enemy of sleep!

For his part, Demane had no quarrel with the body's requirements, sleep least of all. Master Suresh had held the caravan to a cruel pace, with little rest: that, and stoking his metabolic blaze so high, had taken a toll on Demane. The sleepers lay tight-packed around the sorcerous fires. Ceding his spot to someone needing it, Demane spread his groundscloth outside those spheres of brightness and warmth. He sat crosslegged, spear easy to hand, and closed his eyes. Sleet fell on him, steamed away, and more fell. His trance deepened.

Now and again he surfaced. Sleepless and unflagging, the captain could always be seen either pacing, or else startling to wakefulness some night's watchman just beginning to nod. Captain had ridden hardly at all today, although keeping pace on foot at the caravan's forefront had meant flat-out running. Demane thought, as often before: *The littlest children do this.* A baby rages against the eyes closing as if nothing were more hateful. Infants fight for every last instant awake, before being pulled suddenly under, as the captain soon would be, into a vortex of compulsory sleep.

Demane at times could seem to be reading the soul's deepest secrets, but no; it was the body he read. Or that was usually so. Now, in a trance mixing full consciousness with deepest dream, he could glimpse, and even read, a line or two of the soul's secret script. "Hey," he called, beckoning to Captain—who looked first to the sentries: Cumalo, Messed Up, Kazza, Faried, Michelo.

Kazza, in soft falsetto crooning. *I love my wife. She went away from me. What more is there to say?* The other four brothers whose watch it rightly was were all alert too, and pacing up and down. So the captain came over and sat. Say you were a big and burly man who by nature was greatly radiant of heat; then you must learn that your lover would in hot oppressive weathers prefer some distance between you at the hour of sleep, and must learn never to take that move away personally, for it wasn't meant so, not at all. Still, how deeply gratifying, on a raw chill night, to be so jealously pressed against, when you gathered him in snug under a heavy arm. Some other night, Captain would have flung the arm off, overcautious of any touch nearly to the point of giving himself away (for the deeply secretive cannot grasp that protecting your secret too fiercely exposes it). *I'd give my life to set eyes on her again. I loved my wife.* Tonight, Captain's robe was soaked through, and he might be agile, might be quick, but when hawk blew like this, you wanted thickness, not rawboned whipcord—or at least a thick lover. Here, under this arm and against this body, there was vast and soporific warmth.

"Now you free," Demane said, not quite whispering—nor quite awake. "He *been* dead and gone, you know."

Captain sleepily rolled his head on Demane's shoulder to look at him. *What and who are you talking about?*

"That man that tangled fingers in your hair and took away your choice. A prince, I think. No, wait: a king? King-prince. Lion-prince. The Lion."

At Demane's words the captain's face went slack with horror.

"So young back then, you made a bad choice, Captain. *Amante, bailarín, cantante.* My Isa of the Song and Inner Chambers. But it was a very long time ago, wasn't it? Free now, you could make another choice. A good one. For your happiness—"

Captain slapped a hand over Demane's mouth. "*Sorcerer: hush.*"

Demane blinked slowly, and came fully awake. "Sorry, Captain," he said once the reluctant palm allowed him speech. "Sometimes in trance I get to talking out of turn. Did I say what I had no business knowing? Don't let it worry you. I always forget by morning."

Would this prophetic indiscretion put him to flight, drive the captain back out prowling in the cold? No. Though a mind twists and turns, most complicated of all things, the body is a simple creature, and prefers love and comfort, to be where it feels safe. On a freezing night, this one spot right here, *ahhh* . . . Captain fell asleep. Cumalo glanced over. He signed with a hand as folk did back home in the green hills, when the hunt was successful, or some athlete won in the games, or sweethearts were finally wed. *Victory, blessings, congratulations!* Cumalo thankfully did not whoop out the ululating cry as well. Demane smiled, made a shooing gesture, and closed his eyes. He set himself to wake at the final quarter of the night, his watch.

The adept will keep an ear out, even when asleep. Such a big camp never ceases to rustle with a thousand small sounds, but the deepest part of the mind, although sleeping, can sort out that noise which doesn't fit. That one *there*. Bone cracking? Demane opened his eyes and spotted Cumalo, up-Road—and *there*: the sucking withdrawl of deep-embedded fangs?—leaning over at the tent of the merchant Qabr. *Sir? Are you well?* Cumalo whispered. Then from within the tent, a great dark hand swiped out, brushing his brother's belly.

Cumalo toppled backwards, screaming. His innards

rippled greasily forth. Blasted out of sleep, Demane lurched upright, spear in hand: already running. Captain came afoot beside him, passing him by the third stride. A red maw emerged from the tent's flaps, its tusks and teeth all golden-plaqued. They snapped onto Cumalo's shoulder, and bones cracked loudly again, this time such that everyone heard. The tent collapsed just as he and the captain had closed nine and twelve of the twenty strides' distance. Bulk crashed into the nightwood on the east, and all the noise and disturbance of leaves and branches that could be made was made. They'd reached the fallen tent by their sixth heartbeat, but still too late.

The screaming stopped.

Hell broke loose, the whole camp awake. Anarch of the chaos, Messed Up ran to the dark edge of the Road. "Where it at? Where it go?" There, haranguing the wall of brush—though not *entering* it, mind—Messed Up scuttled back and forth. "I just need to *see* that mammerjammer to kill it!" He stabbed his spearpoint into leaves. Silhouetted in orange shadows about the fires, better than one hundred heads raised up, all of them shouting the same, *what just happened, what was that*, the whole camp like a yard full of dogs baying at the night, though the house was already plundered, the thief long fled.

"BE STILL."

Captain's voice smote and crushed the uproar. These words rang out huge and bronze as peals struck off some twelve-ton bell, *STILL* echoing back and subsumed by *BE,* and this rich noise continuing to compound as it diminished in slow opulence.

Struck dumb, no one in the caravan missed Cumalo gag his last. That noise, and the rain hissing into the fires: otherwise the camp was silent. The caravan heard that moan, cut short. From the noctuarium, on its own ground, the great cat purred resonant malice. Captain took the bait and bolted toward the monster, which seemed to lurk in shadows only a few steps off-Road. To step off here, however, was to cross planets and millennia; for all the worlds were in flux, and poised to change on the moment for anyplace in the wild depths of time and space. A trap: to fling any pursuit into a random point of infinity—

Demane lunged, catching Captain's shins, and bore them both down to the ground.

"Stop, Isa, *stop*. I couldn't catch him like this, at night under a cloudy sky. No way you can!" Demane brought his weight to bear, pinning the thrashing man beneath him. "Tiger killed him already, and will eat *you too*." Wildly Captain fought to rise, but Demane was stronger. "By *day*, Isa, in the *sun*. When we can see the signs. We *both* go and catch him *then*, that jukiere!"

The captain's frenzy stilled. One of his hands touched Demane's wrist and, suddenly by some wrestler's black magic, Demane found himself stunned and on the bottom, Captain on top. He got off and to his feet, looking blankly down—but accepted an outstretched hand, to pull Demane up beside him.

The caravan watched its two best. No differently would children watch mama and papa squabble in the parlor as the house went up, the heat intolerable, and fire washing over the walls: desperately hanging on to every word, for their lives depended on this outcome. Firelight flickering on wet skin picked out the dark crowd in orange glimmers. Then a pyre came crashing down upon itself, and grown men gave the shrieks of merest girls. There was sheepish silence afterwards, in which they heard heavy meat dragged away through thicket and underbrush. The bitter wind already was warming and dying down. Hot raindrops fell more and more among the cold, and soon only hot.

They drew the merchant Qabr out feet first through the slashes in the tent's back side. Nor were any wounds to be seen on his feet or legs, his robe all unstained, not one mark upon his torso: such that, at first, it seemed the merchant might emerge in their arms alive, only in a swoon. Then a stir of condolence moved through the littler brotherhood of merchant boys. The pale and dark nephews, one a fifth son, the other a seventh, had become sole and sudden inheritants of two fortunes. By their grief and its abandon, however, they'd rather had the uncles than coin. Below the neck, Qabr's body was pristine and unharmed. His head, caught and crushed by long teeth, was a torn and punctured bag, slopping bloody curd and shards of skull.

"For *this* we pay you full-weights of gold, Captain Isa Johnny?" Master Suresh l'Merqerim declaimed like a politician in the marketplace. "That some bitching whore out of Hell should come and go, butchering us merchants with impunity?" He gave them high-flown hands, outraged finger-pointing, the whole bit. "How will you make this good? Two excellent men dead already, *two*! And a brother."

"No one else will die," sang the captain to the caravan *basso profundissimo*, that voice which is palpable in teeth and bones. "At daybreak, I'll go into the Wildeeps and kill the jooker tiger."

That, obviously, wanted amending: "Me and Captain, both," Demane said.

The night was raw no longer, now sultry, without nip to the breeze. Still, an outcry went up when Demane moved to quench the fires. So he left the lights burning. In that hellish heat, son huddled beside father, nephew by uncle, brother with brother. The caravan had stopped quite early for the night; day therefore took its sweet time coming. A few more tired than afraid succumbed to sleep, and Captain among them. Several times, as a swimmer drowns, he nodded up to wakefulness, but slipped always back under, until his head came up no more.

Man or woman, everyone in the green hills was permitted three days after any death during which to howl out their grief. On the fourth day you had to begin picking up your responsibilities again. Here, though... a tight jaw, a little red-eyed blinking, was meant to be the extent of it. *Cumalo!* Not being made for such noiseless tears, Demane cheated, storing away his grief.* He

---

*   You will knock, and a sharp-eyed old man answer. "Yes?" He'll look you over and see what you hold: a fist-size pouch, fat with coin. "What do you want?"

"To talk to the lady of the warrior Cumalo, please. I was a friend of his."

You see the elder grasps at once what news you bring, but he'll bridle and bluster anyway, in the tedious way of northern men. "No call to go bothering my daughter. And it ain't proper, nohow, you calling on a married lady. Speak your piece to me."

Not to bandy words on some doorstep will you have come fifteen hundred miles, nor yet will you have learned to fully bank the fires of godhead—still there will be flares—and this with nothing said of divinity's concomitants: the great arrogance, the small sufferance of fools. "Bring me before his wife, little man, and you'd best not make me say it again."

Through successive dark rooms you will follow toward a doorway full of white glare, the old man calling *Janisse, somebody come for you!*

breathed in the measured way Aunty had taught him, and opened his senses fully to the surroundings, allowing his observation of every stimulus to hone ever finer and more granular until he became a sentinel unbeholden to thought or feeling, only alert, only watching.

The sleepless faced the east. And hardly did dawn extend a rosy finger to caress the sky before Master Suresh crossed the mud from one of the lowburning fires. He made to kick Captain's foot and waken him, but thought better and checked, seeing Demane's face. There, something deep—*fell* and deep—came very near the surface. The Sorcerer shrugged and the captain's head rolled up-

---

Sun shall beat upon a courtyard. Hen and pullets scratch the dust. Two *olivos* grow ancient and gnarled. Mother wash child.

The woman, her skirts wet, lifts a towel-wrapped baby into her arms from gray water filling a tub. She's taller than you, long-armed, smelling of benignity and fatigue: everything as Cumalo described. It's the sight of the baby, however, that undoes you. Three years old and very much alive, she has the same heavy-lidded eyes, same untroubled air, as the dead man who was her father.

"Ma'am . . . ," you'll say, holding out the little bag of full-weights. "Your husband . . ." Then your voice clots, and your eyes spill the first tears they will have shed for poor Cumalo; Janisse shaking her head slowly at first, and then with vehemence. These will be the gesture and instant comprehension of someone who's always known she'd have to hear what's about to be said. The child, too young to understand, sleepily sucks her thumb, looking between weeping mother, weeping stranger.

on his shoulder—he jerked awake. They stood. From the gore-spatter in the mud up-Road, and thence into the greenish murk of the Wildeeps, they followed the drag-trail of Cumalo's body.

Whereof no one dared speak but all did wonder, that among them a single disciple should be held, and he alone, in deeper confidence. Once in bitter jest a brother called that preferred disciple the Lover: hence the name, not his own, which comes down to us. *None save for the Lover accompanied the Patriarch* upon the unknown errand when nights were dark, nor did anyone see them again before the morning . . .

from *Commentaries on Holy Recitature*

Seventh of Seven

. . . into a place of deciduous gigantism, the air too rich and stinking of sulfur, of ozone, some unearthly black snow—ash, rather—sifting down: another world, and bright midmorning here. Muttering *earthquake*, muttering *pyroclastic surge*, the ground underfoot thrummed. "You near about beat," Demane said, urgency giving his tone an edge. "Snatch that off your head, and you won't be."

Captain glanced over his shoulder at the Road. A few from the caravan, like children standing before a mirror, gaped blindly back at him.

"They cain't see you," Demane snapped. "It's another world from there. And we gotta go—so, *right now*, Isa." To stand atop a supervolcano, nine months gravid and about to blow, was nerve-wracking. "Quick!"

Not so quick: just a headscarf, but there have been many shy virgins who shimmied from their drawers more boldly. Uncovered, Captain's hair flashed once blindingly (Demane—eyes closed, a hand thrown up to shield them further—saw that red flare) and then, gorging widely upon EMR, the heliophages dimmed and darkened past matte, past black, to the fuliginous. Some other time, Demane would have lingered over this sight, for it was wonderful to see how Captain's eyes, bloodshot and purple-shadowed, instantly clarified, and every sign of fatigue and endurance sloughed from him, exchanged for the fretful antsiness of a superb and rested athlete. But they were standing on a continent that was about to halve in size. Demane rechecked the spoor and trail, seized the captain's hand, and flung him forward through dense foliage into the next world, himself right behind . . .

. . . pulling the captain second to take point himself, as soon as the leaves snapped closed behind them. "Come here," he said; Captain came into his arms. "Close your eyes." Demane's pores drenched them both, misting aroma herbaceous and evergreen. The air around them cleared, clouds of midge and mosquito falling away.

The captain screwed up his face, blinking away tears. "Ah! Stinks like rosemary."

Nothing would scent their approach or passage now, either by nose or tongue. They would still, of course, have to watch out, and take care about making noise. And on, to the next world . . .

Had he gone home to the green hills, Demane would have seen men dressed sensibly for the heat, women walking boldly about their business; he could again have

expressed himself in the mothertongue, and stopped trying to uphold foreign ways. Going off-Road into the
Wildeeps was a joyful homecoming of another kind. Only in the most perilous wilderness could wild power safely unleash itself.

Monsters filled the forest. Twice Demane tore away
at a dead run and Captain paced him, half a step behind.
Twice again, he held them both flat to the ground, while
through the jungle nearby some colossus passed unseen,
the earth and trees quaking with fourfooted booms, and
they lying under the thickets, with breath held, or scarcely breathing.

Only one of them could perceive the wizard cat's
wake. Only one of them could track the sign under leafy
darkness, through mist and rain, and see them safely past
every peril. And so no talk, no conflict, entered into who
would boldly lead, who meekly follow. The trail took
them as much from glade to glade as between worlds.
Aunty would have been proud. Demane learned miracles
she'd never taught, and learned them on his feet, at speed.

. . . breathing in the minutely floating odorants left
by the jukiere's passage. Molecules mixed on his tongue
with secretions of the pineal gland—which, in the
Wildeeps, was no longer a rare ichor to eke out in meager
drops. Here, his third eye abundantly replenished itself.
The wonders he could work! Demane spat. The hot ex-

pectoration seethed onto the path ahead, and the way to the next world opened. An effluvious gate . . .

Even in deepest shadow of the understorey Demane was aware when infinities of scent suddenly vanished away, and myriad new odors bloomed over the space of a single step. Families of flora would regress to emergent infancy or advance to atrophied old age. Brethrens of beasts disappeared, and came back anew in strange variants. Nothing remained the same over distances, except the wizard's vagrant trail. As the worlds changed, so did the times—by leaps of innumerate years: millennia of millennia, if such numbers existed.

. . . careful! *There*—a toad, beetle-small and searingly green as pond scum, crept on the path ahead. It so reeked of murderous fumes that Demane, though all but unpoisonable, had no wish to touch it. For another man to brush the tiny creature even glancingly would kill him on the spot. With the butt of his spear, Demane gouged the dirt and slung the virid speck, mud-engulfed, off the path where Captain's foot (half naked in a sandal) would step a moment after his own . . .

. . . and the broadleaf canopy sealed above them. Though late morning, it was midnight on the forest floor—light in plenty, of course, for the eyes of a child of Tower TSIMtsoa. All this while, and from world to world, Captain had dogged Demane's heels with the same lightly treading mimicry of a shadow. Now, he shook his hand loose; for just ahead the black-on-black brocade of the jungle shredded, with the tatters admitting sunlight. The captain went to this expanse of dappled foliage and, like some man parched with thirst ducking his face into a pool of water, thrust his head through the leaves to take some sun. According to the spoor, the jukiere had also stopped here not so long ago. Demane stepped up to the prospect beside Captain.

They stood atop a forested bluff, which commanded a view of valley, river running through, and surrounding ridges. At their feet the abrupt slope dropped off into depthless tangles of weed that overgrew the valley from end to end. This world or time was far ancestral to their own, Demane judged. Infusing the scent-drenched air was not one whiff of plant or animal known to him. Across the lush weedfields, in the middle distance, flowed a sludgy river. Sheersided crags, facelike, closed the valley in: the cliffs as smooth as cheeks, the dark bosky heights suggesting hair. One sight held both men captive. Sized so as to beggar comparison, some great vast beast extended its sinuous neck from the muddy waters of the river. If not the whole, could a much smaller part of its body be likened, then? The head was elephantine, and swept up to tree height in order to chew, and then down, to snatch immense tracts of greenery from the riverbank. And the beast's head was minute beside the forehaunches which rose tremendously above the water's surface.

"Something's strange, D." Captain murmured so softly he must have guessed the range of Demane's hearing. "Have you seen how the forest keeps changing . . . ?" He took a step almost into full sunlight.

"Yeah—" The breeze shifted: charged with carnivorous reptile. Demane lunged, seized the captain, and drew him back under good cover.

"Tiger? Nearby?" He asked almost without sound. But Demane fiercely shook his head, and covered the captain's mouth. He lifted his little finger to point down toward the river.

The leviathan fed. Hard by, some new prodigy erupted from the depths of weeds. *This*, by teeth and claws, was no eater of plants! From subtle creeping the monster launched upwards into the air. That leap could not have spanned half a league, surely, however far it seemed— some great distance, though: powered by hugely muscled legs many times the size of its short withered arms. Off the shore of the river there was a muddy island. . . . Ah, no: that was the weed-eater's back! There, the other landed, claws furrowing through flesh; the fanged jaws snapped down for a mouthful that could have champed a rhino in two. An unspeakable live butchery commenced.

Here, it would help to have seen the Assumption of
the Towers. Such a cataclysm! Tongues of fire licked the
clouds; eruptions of steam such as the gods in bright as-
cent saw blot the sphere below them; tsunami, world-
wide; and the isle itself dissolving as does a clump of
wet sand, held in a child's cupped palm which she then
ducks, open, under the froth of an incoming wave. Or it
would help to know as much of shock and awe as those
farflung few, survivors of the long night of dragons, when
the Assassin of Cities, Rain of Fire, Lightstorm, Death
from Above, Utter Ruin, and Torrent of Thunderbolts
brought low the empire of Daluça, capital and colonies,
burning and blasting the flower of mortal civilization.
But without a cheek or brow brushed by edgefeathers of
the archangel's wings, while you stood a witness to some-
such enormity and from so near, what hope of understanding what they felt?

This is what they saw:

The excavations of the carnivore sent up blasts like
storm surge against a rocky headland. Oceanic and salty:
though these waters were scarlet blood. Honks of the
leviathan cracked back from the cliffs of the valley, echoing, and the outflow of its gore purpled the brown river.
The breeze ripened, coating Demane's tongue and filling
his nose with odor and savor of snake's blood, snake's
meat. He could hardly make out the captain's mélange

of earthling and stardust, though in his very arms. From roosts in the basalt visages—from eyes and nostrils—shadows of greatwinged manikins launched into the upper void.

The sky was cloudless and the river without fog, but throughout the valley a misty pall floated in the middle of the air. Those huge birds wheeled down from the cliff faces, down through suspended vapor, down into the lower clarity. There, they took shape as feathered crocodiles. Half the monstrous flock was bigger and more gaudily colored than the other. One by one the raptors, sized like little men, alighted on the bountiful carcass. Soon dozens of them sawed away with barbed bills. The flux of the river foamed pink and white around the behemoth as submerged scavengers began to feed.

Lord of them all, the twolegged dragon glutted itself, and lesser monsters scattered whereverfrom it wished to bite. Even the rocs, scaly titans, and river sharks couldn't strip the meat off that mountain in the time the two of them stood watching; still, substructures of skeleton, like support beams of a palace under construction, began to come into view.

The primordial awe ebbed from Demane first. His hand still lightly cupped the captain's mouth. When he slid it away Captain turned vague, astonished eyes on him. They were the last shade of brown before black, color of coffee, and just now neither grim nor sad but wonderstruck. He was all soft-side-up for a change. And unplucked there on his mouth were kisses like lowhanging fruit, ripe and deeply pink. But the beloved too has extraordinary senses; he scents importunity. "The tiger," Captain murmured and, blinking himself fully alert, spoke a word chilling even to the hottest lover: "Cumalo."

Demane turned back to the depths of the forest. "Well, come on with you, then."

A season ago, Demane walked in low spirits through the market of Philipiya. On that afternoon, rather than pass by, he stopped at the mercenaries' post. There was a man crying as usual: "*Warriors! Brave men! Wealth!*" Beside the crier stood another man, who smelled richly of extraterrestrial heritage. Demane went over. The one who cried put questions to him; Demane answered, his eyes on the other all the while, addressing him. Alumnus of many wars by the beads round his neck, and speechless in a black robe, black headscarf, there was no reason to believe the man other than mute—not deaf, though, for he attended Demane's answers closely. Then they sparred for a brief bout. Demane spoke. "You staying over in a travelers' barracks? They kind of nasty, ain't they? You ought to come with me." However this man answered, Demane knew his life was about to change. "I got good rooms in the amir's palace. What's your name, anyway?"

The man dismissed the crier with a glance. And then for the first time Demane heard Captain's voice:

"I'm Isa of Sea-john, Demane. But if you come with the caravan, you must call me Captain."

Wait, now: hush, Demane thought to himself. *He's bitterly ashamed of his voice. So you'd better not say, 'Your talk is like a song. I never heard anything so beautiful in my life!'*

"Where's Sea-john at, Captain?"

"It's the borough where foreigners live, down in Great Olorum. Call me Isa when it's just us."

"I don't know that place, Olorum, either." Demane said. They were crossing out of the market. The crowd among the vegetable stands convulsed, women with baskets fleeing toward the wharves: the late fishermen were coming in. Demane caught the captain's hand and even when the jostling rush had passed kept hold of it.

"Look, Isa, I don't get how you all do it here," he said, "but I want to . . . love you. Understand me?"

The captain looked sideways at him and did not quite smile. But the handclasp lost neutrality and became erotic, a sign of something sure. For this man, Demane decided—on the spot, at that moment—he would stick it out, cross continents, do whatever love required. Captain said, "I understand you just fine." The sublime low throb of his whisper!

Day after next, midmorning, he departed Philipiya with the caravan of Master Suresh l'Merqerim—without a word of goodbye to either the amir, or that harried ruler's spoiled son. Menials know all that happens in a palace, however. And so two marble-swabbers, some laundresses, and a run-fetch boy were able to variously report having seen him leave in the company of an Olo-rumi mercenary, quite thin, unusually tall. And though Demane left behind emptied room, abandoning not one fine rich robe, nor the smallest gaud his patron had given him, the reports of all these menials coincided: as he'd shown up, so did he leave—in the altogether, and carry-ing just that same ratty little bag.

———

Demane waited until he drew a breath smacking of car-rion, and then said, "Let me see the point of your spear." Captain presented his spear. Demane pulled the shaft lower and pricked a finger on the tip, smearing his blood so that it glazed the spearleaf entirely.

"Demane . . . ?" the captain sang low.

"With the magis' greatwork, any knife, spear, rock or whatever can hurt a creature spinning on the Towers' left while you're on the Road. But off-Road, you need, uh . . . a sorcerer's blessing. As long as you can see me, or me you, that spear's good against the jukiere. All right?"

Captain nodded. And soon thereafter, in his nostrils too the reek of putrescence began to bloom and burn. A dull buzzing roar began to rise: countless thousands of flies, still at some distance. The captain's face assumed its severest aspect, braced against a stench that could be little short of emetic for him.

Demane whispered, "If you need some help standing the smell . . ."

Manfully—foolishly—Captain shook his head.

A clearing. Flies frenzied in the air. The sun shone down upon a massive stump, truncated by lightning-strike about ten feet above their heads. The cataclysmic fall of this adolescent redwood had smashed a long glade through the jungle. The gap in the canopy admitted light by which all the boneyard's horrors could be seen: several dozen bodies, human and swine.

Some butcher had not judged them different meats. For with intimate promiscuity cadaver of man and carcass of pig lay strewn together, in every attitude and condition of death. A few freshkill, some fallen to bones. Most bodies in intermediate states: well and thoroughly dead—liquescent, bloated, purpling—and yet quick with life too, such were the worms, the seething coverlet of flies. Disjointed limbs were littered round about; and everywhere underfoot, clots of errant pork, strange gobbets, ribbons of flesh. Bad as these sights were, for Captain the smell could only be worse. Breathe by mouth if he liked, but the gases of decomposition would be stinking to point of savor. Every breath over his tongue would taste of vile broth.

Cravenly, Demane invoked arts to which Captain had no recourse. He kept raw emotion at bay, his sensibilities more nearly animal than a man's.

As Aunty had once with him, he murmured and gestured: " . . . see how the wizard's two-times picky? Us or pigs: nothing else. Ah, look at that one there. The way the jukiere take only two or three good bites? It won't fill up on just one body, they *always* waste. It is a [mainstay of entropic necromancy] . . . part of their bad juju . . ."

And there was Cumalo. The cat had kicked sticks, leaves, dirt over the body. Out from under this mess extended their brother's legs and sandaled feet. Demane and the captain approached. A half-dozen crows saucily dawdled, gouging out last bits, cawing complaints at them, before at last taking to wing and scattering down to other feasts. With the butt of his spear Demane knocked aside the shoddy cairn. Facedown, Cumalo lay atop swatches of his clawed-apart robe. The rigid fingers of one hand clenched about some final treasure, which Demane crouched to recover: a knucklebone die. Iridescent flies resettled along the white and red-gummed exposure of his pelvis and femur bones. The back of the body, apart from the mauled shoulder, and the neck, lolling askew—"You see, Captain? They kill by choking"—remained whole. Demane swung the butt of his spear toward bushes a few long strides away, under which were heaped the ropes and bags of their brother's entrails, pulled out whither the taint couldn't turn the meat faster. Demane paused doubtfully. Did he belabor? Was he speaking with strange dispassion? Both of these? He peeked sidelong.

Captain sweated copiously. His face was drawn taut, immobile but for his upper lip quivering in a nauseated sneer. Abruptly he staggered back, bowed forcibly: retching forth a mouthful of water, and then heaving dryly several times. There was no reckless courage in this world— no hardihood, no manful strength, no mad feats on fields of battle—that would keep down the gorge in the bone-yard of a jukiere. Demane allowed bitter citrus attar to flood his mouth. He pulled the captain upright and forced a deep strange kiss. The agile mollusc of his tongue lapped over and under Captain's, and then around and up into either nostril. Once let go, Captain sucked in a long breath and rubbed at his nose, while the tart potency stunned his sense of taste and smell. He grunted—hornlike, tuneful—and nodded ungracious thanks.

The men this side of the continent didn't like their weakness watched, so Demane turned away, studying the ground. He wandered, and hunkered down next to prints lately pressed into bloody muck. The noisome airs and flies' whining roar blunted the fine acuity of his nose and ears; but sight had all its sharpness. Something was bothering him about the sign, these prints; what? When Demane next glanced over, Captain had found the remains of the merchant Iuliano. Demane looked down again, trying to grasp what eluded him. Jukiere tracks, no doubt about that: the spread and shape of toes, the forefoot polydactyl where the claws didn't retract . . . And this was sure enough the boneyard of a jukiere, all the waste of half eaten bodies, and yet, *something*—

A dry stick cracked, nearby.

"Here it come!" Demane shouted.

The great cat roared, just out of sight in the trees. Closer to the noise, Captain bolted toward it, spear in hand. Demane had followed only three steps when the jukiere broke cover and streaked across his path, crashing westward into the brush, though the captain had gone north. "West, Captain, *west*!" Demane shouted, while turning to give chase.

His attention narrowed to matters of pursuit. The

great cat surged around the trunks of trees, plunged through black densities of brush. Demane held his best sprint without tiring; but faster over the short distance, the jukiere kept easily ahead. The ground began to grade upwards, and there Demane found himself gaining with every step. He burst into sunlight where the slope cleared to treelessness between thickets. Only a short lunge away up the embankment, the tiger whirled at bay. It leapt back downwards.

Male. The bearded ruff, those thickly gnarled fore-shoulders. Downcurved tusks a full foot long—

Demane moved with instinctual speed. Planting his spear's butt against the ground, he leveled its point toward the cat, and braced for impact. The shaft jarred deeply into leaf-rot. Demane ducked from scrabbling claws, yanking with all his might. Impaled, the jukiere vaulted overhead and on down the embankment. The spear tore loose from his grasp, he himself somersaulting downward one time, before arresting his descent with a snatched handhold of rank vine.

Only in movement could the jukiere be seen. When still, the creature's brindled coat merged with the jungle's greenish light and shadow. The fur of its flanks and back was mature evergreen, dark-stippled as if muddy. Its fur hung thick and longer along throat and underbelly, new-grass-color, white with age at the fringes. The spear had broken the joint of the great cat's left foreshoulder, and there was lodged. The cat stepped its right forepaw and great weight onto the shaft, but the wood held, unbending. Not would it ever break, so long as Demane lived. Batting at the shaft, the jukiere worried at it until the spear fell free.

Demane kicked against slick crushed greenery and mud. His hand clutching at vines, his feet gaining purchase neither to move upwards nor to stand. Wind rose at his back, blowing to the jukiere and past him came a windborne power spinning counter to his own, TSIMtsoa. The hot air became foul with maneater's funk, with bowels torn bloodily open; the wind rang with such cries as quarry gives when caught, when eaten alive: the squeals and screams, a rare decipherable word, *help*. As the jukiere pulled strength from the Wildeeps, this shrieking miasma whipped about it. The red hole in the tiger's shoulder ceased to bleed, and fleshed over, and the nude flesh furred. That fourth paw came down gingerly. The cat put confident weight on it.

He could do the same, Demane saw: spinning the power as TSIM rather than TSOA. A chrism of bright sun poured down, and humanity dropped off him like a cloak. His imperfect flesh ripped itself inside-out with the rise to perfection, *Not piece by piece, all at once: metamorphosis is like death,* as he welcomed the change he'd fought off since crossing over into the Wildeeps *in that it ruptures mind from body. By grace of the blood, though, your consciousness can cohere into flesh and bone after transformation. If you're strong enough, if you don't vanish into the void. Only you can judge whether the gods' heritage is enough expressed in you to bring you back past throwing off human shape. No one can tell you that; only you will know. For a talisman, gather thoughts of what matters most to you.*

—All mine shall live so long as I do: I spear these desperadoes in defense of my brothers. For clumsy little Walead; for Faedou who took a knife to the leg; for Ca—

Join together these precious lights as a beacon, and the gathered shining of your treasures will call you back from the fall into death.

—Aunty needed one of us to pick up the burden. Somebody has to. I'm not leaving the green hills to hurt you, whom I love. I go because I'm the last one left who can—

Becoming the stormbird is as easy for me as you put on your mantle for holidays; I've got the trick of it. I think you can get it too. But don't hurt yourself, Mountain Bear. A heart like yours or mine works miracles best doing for others. So wait on your cause. Or on love. His talons, rootlike, sank lengthily into the mud. Demane came back within a heartbeat: winged and leatherskinned, now. He was no longer a couple inches shy of six feet but just past seven, with hands and maw full of knives.

The tiger made to spring, low and hunch-shouldered. Its sooty lips curled up, the ribbon of its tongue lolling. Fiery pinpricks glowed in its wizard-eyes.

Demane fell back a step, and another man's last thoughts became his own:

Four lines of black ice slit his belly to tatters. His first scream owed more to fright and surprise, not yet wholly to pain. Hot wet weight slopped down his lap and legs, the living burden of his body suddenly lightened. He thought only to—*run!* But already too weak, he fell sprawling about to shout *Help! Captain! Sorcerer!* But agony forestalled any such outcry: fingerlength spikes drove through his shoulder. The socket burst, collarbone crumbled, and bony wing of his back shattered. Great rough strength slung him through the mud. The bonfires on the Road went dark. He saw nothing, felt only the scratching smack of leaves, and weird soft loops entangling his legs. He could scream, he could kick—there was nothing else left to do. A gamey fetor lunged at him, *hot*, faceward. Last act in life, he got up his elbow, somehow, into the way. Almighty teeth savaged that arm, and folded it down throttlingly around his own throat. There was no breath and no breath and still there was none, and still none. You could count these last slow final blinks on the fingers of one hand, nor need all five. Drugged sleep dampened the fires of his terror. This world ebbing, the enigma burgeoned . . .

Cumalo died. Demane woke, toppling backwards under the weight of the wizard. Claws raked down his chest unable to score his hide. Fangs closed on his impenetrable throat. Stronger, he tore himself free of the crushing maw. The evil wind blew again, and the wizard's green brindled coat went black and bright as a thundercloud, its fur blazing and freezing in restless patches. Crackling flashes snapped between the hot and cold spots. Demane struck again and again, with all his strength, but his bladed fingers turned on the jukiere's flesh, and frost bit his hands. Fire scorched them. Where was his spear? The absent gods had left that spear for this very purpose: killing jukiere. Where *was* it? Neither talon nor claw drawing any blood, they traded blows, impervious to each other. The cat snarled, and Demane husked the strange roar that bespoke his anger in this shape.

And still the Wildeeps went without master, its numina inexhaustible and unclaimed: so draw *again*. Drink!

Demane drank. His galled and ashen hands blackened, sleek and whole. *When I was even younger than you, my mother came back from a long time away—but not in the flesh. She came as light, only to say goodbye. I think she'd gone too far or too deep working some great miracle, and so lost the route back to humanity.* He batted the jukiere off its feet and against a great tree, which burst to flinders, the splintered wood into flames. Back broken, the jukiere tried to rise, front paws scrabbling. Time to finish it. Laying his talons point-on-point to make spears of his hands, Demane winged toward the cat. *Which drink would be one too far? When was the last line crossed?* Already?

In unison Demane and the wizard reached to partake of the Wildeeps—and neither could. Back and forth, they wrestled for ascendancy, the jukiere winning. It surged to its feet. On patches of its fur the action of minute particles ceased, or nearly so; but the hot patches blazed with diametric heat. When Demane speared down a hand to impale the cat, his hand burst into flames. The talons shattered on contact. Seething eruptions of blisters went up his arm. Body and wings: his whole self began to smoke. He crashed to earth. Trees—all the vegetation roundabout—crisped to black, the cinders falling to white ash, and the ash too burning. In another moment, some patch of the jukiere's fur, infinitely cold, would meet parallel fires, and the resulting discharge . . .

One last drink, then: nothing measured, as much as he could hold. Everything. The talons that had broken regrew, the intact hardened to adamant, and then tapered finer than a hairsbreadth. He flung that hand around, knifing into flesh, cleaving between ribs. The wizard halted the talons' plunge with its whole visceral will; its stormy fur went dark. They strained against one another.

And still Demane drank, as the river below drinks when the dam above has broken. *"The gods travel as light,"* she said. *"I'm joining the Tower in the purissime. You and the children come up when you can."* A star falling the wrong way: that's how she left me. It is possible for one to win and yet lose—or the other to lose, and die, but take out the enemy too. The jukiere stopped its struggles and instead lunged, with jaws fully agape, forward onto the impaling talons. The tiger's fangs and tusks, death-limned and aglow with every mustered erg of necromancy, would for a last act snap shut upon Demane's head.

There's another, deeper metamorphosis, I think. No, I can't tell you anything about that one. We'll learn it by ourselves, if we ever do. You and me both.

Demane spat forth a black glimmering particulate which unmade everything it touched. Each annihilative spark vanished in the instant of unmaking until, headless, the jukiere fell—*stormbird triumphant!* Demane roared as strength upon strength poured unstoppably into him. His skin took light, sublimating off his bones, and they themselves began to glow, turning to hot gas. Up or away he was carried at great speed across darkness into some dense, rushing, many-layered radiance. In the tidal light he found his tier among winged brethren, who gladly made room for him. And having gathered him up, glory deepened to sweep him from the shores of Earth back toward infinity, but *she* caught his arm. The woman had the quiet poise of Demane's elder sister, a muscled shape like his own, Aunty's stature, the ageless looks of his parents: so that they all must share close blood, though who this stranger was Demane couldn't guess. "Stay longer than a moment, boy, and there's no going back. Will you let that jukiere take over the Wild Depths?" Hard to care about terrestrial trivia when the gods of TSIMTSOA called from only a little farther upstream . . . "Wait, boy—*wait!* Didn't you leave somebody behind? What was it you kept meaning to say to him?"

—*But you hate this life, Captain; you know you do. So if you promised ole Suresh this last journey, then come away with me after we get to Great Olorum. All this is so easy in the green hills. There, you and me could*—

Demane broke from the light, and fought his way back down toward mortality.

———————

"Ha!" Demane laughed; the sonority was palpable in his belly, his bones, his teeth. "I can *feel* that one. My teeth jumping." Next, Isa gave a rich whistle too high and fast to credit from human lips, except that Demane lay there watching the feat, listening rapt. It was like a bitty songbird's welcome to the sunrise. "Now *that* one's pretty, right there. But say again? It went by so fast, I couldn't catch one word." Other voices too, none of them any strain at all for him, every one equally his own. And at last Demane exclaimed, "No, no, no: *that* one! I like that one best."

"This is a woman's voice, you know."

"Is it? Beautiful on anybody. Just seem like it fit you, that's all. But I could see a man or woman, really."

"No, it's a woman's voice. *Deepwaters,** we say in Sea-john. Men's start just a little bit deeper, and not so rich. I like this one, too. A long time ago, I used to . . . well, that stuff doesn't matter now. All right, pop—for you. But only when we're alone, you hear? On caravan I have to speak much lower; for respect, so brothers will follow. This one's still too high."

The weight of the jukiere towed him to his knees, and from there sprawled facedown in its clammy fur. Just a man again, with little more than any man's strength, De-

---

* Tiefer alt. A voice to sing the pale sour out of lemons, sing them luscious orange; as much the sensations of *eros* on the body as mere sound in the ears.

mane couldn't shift it. The wizard was *heavy*. Its eyes had turned to glass, its flesh to a quarter ton of clay. He braced his heels to the headless carcass and, pulling back against the wet-suck of the wound, dredged forth his arm. It came free badly scored along its length, all gashed and chewed by splintered bone.

He cradled his torn arm to him. A sip of power from the Wildeeps would heal these injuries. But could he hold himself to that, just a sip, or would another apocalyptic binge rapture him beyond the sky, newest and least godling of the radiant pantheons? Well before noon on the day he decides to go dry, the drunkard already finds himself trembling. That Demon whispers: *You can handle it. A little taste. Just get your lips wet.*

No . . . he'd better let the wounds stand.

Captain was nowhere in sight, and nowhere close by: must have gotten turned around. He'd know to go back and wait at the boneyard. And just how long would he abide there before striking out alone? In space, it was only a quarter league east to reach the Road, but there were several millennia to cross in time . . . Demane cut off that thought. He fetched his spear from where it had fallen. The captain, no fool, would wait longer than the short while that had passed.

Demane jogged back the way he'd come.

Just a man again, child of TSIMTSOA? Knifesharp

leaves struck him always flat-side, never edged; thickets thinned for him, and fanged thornbrakes, pulled aside, whipped back and missed, points always angled to his advantage: the briars caught by greenery, or broken off or blunted. Any other man—just a man—would wonder that all the rotten bits of debris, the sticks and rocks underfoot, kept presenting only soft or smooth-side-up to his soles. But His Majesty, thinking deep thoughts, was oblivious to the scramble of his countless servitors. Demane had yet to learn he'd never be quit of godhead having now put it on.

Ahead was a tree. Approaching it Demane's step slowed, his knees made weak by sudden understanding. Jukiere piss-sign had splashed all over the tree's roots, wet only a day ago: at most two. But the scent didn't belong to the jukiere cooling stiff and flyblown on the embankment behind him. There was another, nor aged nor male. She was in fresh youth, just a few days from throwing a litter of fiends. Demane ran.

———

Soft fingers held him, a damp cloth wiping. He blinked sleepily.

Back from bathing, Isa looked up from these ministrations. "It's true, what you said. But you don't know the brothers yet, Demane. Somebody's got to look out for them." He tossed the cloth aside, beyond the sheets. "It's in you to learn fast. So after we come to Great Olorum, take over the captaincy if you want." Isa smiled. "*I'd* follow you. You'd be ten times better at it than I am."

Demane sat up, caught him, pulled him down. "You just now met me in the market. Where do you get all this?"

"I'm telling you, D., you've got a hero's shine on you. Just as bright as anybody I ever knew. I know it when I see it."

"Me? Naw; I'm no hero. You got me mixed with yourself, maybe. You been in big battles, ain't you? And wasn't you over there in that war?" Demane tapped the red coral and white shell necklace Isa wore, one among many, and many-colored. Isa gave him no reply, only a glance that said too much, or said it too vaguely, for interpretation (his finger tracing vascular bulk and striation of Demane's shoulder and arm). *Over there*, yes: and marshal of the campaign, too. But Demane would only learn this much later on, when the knowledge could make no difference. "Me, I don't know nothing about big combat or command. You the one."

"I know what I'm good for. Believe that, Demane. And I know that if you keep up your wandering, this whole continent will know your name one day."

Demane smiled peaceably, settling deeper in the pillows; his fastidious new lover sprawled half on, half beside him. If the point was to please him, then Isa could just as well have lain beside him until morning, smelling funky and used. But during two days in bed, with only a quick step out here and there to wolf some meal in the market, Isa always found an imperceptible moment to slip off and bathe, between each time they made love and next. And he never spoiled the afterglow, nor lingered long enough to be missed. What timing! A supernatural gift for love, you'd almost have said. So off south—tomorrow morning!—over the burning rocky hills, across the weeks-wide desert, and finally to some distant, meridonal city called Great Olorum? Sure, all right. This man's reverent touch, his *vox seraphica*; the beard that looked to be coarse, but was downy to the touch . . . what was there to complain of here?

"I was wrong about one thing, though."

"Yeah, whas that?"

"I thought you were going to be a hard man. You know—mean to me."

"What?" Demane frowned. "But why would you go with somebody like that?" He sat up on an elbow. "*Why*—?"

"Aw, don't get upset, pop. I'm *glad* you're kind." If you'd distract a lion? Throw some bloody steak. "Hey!"

Captain slipped a smooth long leg across Demane's lap to straddle him. "Ready to go again? Uh huh, I *see*. We've got to make sure you get plenty now, because I can't let you have it like this on the road . . ."

Overcast warred with blue in the windy firmament. It was sweltering, not long past noon. Two heaps of ash remained of the night's bonfires, red cinders winking in the white powder. A half dozen burros wandered on the black earth verge, heads in the green while they stood in the mud of the Road. The caravan had decamped, all save for a few brothers—three, four, or five—prayerfully huddled at center-Road. Past the distortion of the veil, the brotherly shapes wavered as if seen through heat shimmer; only the faintest trace of their wet and unwashed humanity came to his nose, their voices remote echoes in his ears. He tossed his burden onto the Road. The grisly decapitation of the monster struck the ground not far from where they knelt in strange vigil, and the head rolled closer still. Five dim forms rose, making noises that were murmurs to him, too faint to make sense of. Walead?—yes; it was Walé who crouched down again to poke at the gore, the tusks, the tongue lolling over the sharp teeth of the gaping mouth.

Xho Xho ran up to the edge of the Road where Demane stood like a revenant on the threshold.

"Where the captain went?" the boy asked. "Why you don't come out of the trees, Sorcerer?"

"I cain't, Xho."

"Hey, you watch out," Kazza called. "Hear me, Xho Xho? Watch out now!"

The other brothers kept a warier distance. Something wasn't right. The Sorcerer was barked over with half-dried mud, jellied gore, twigs, and bits of leaves. Blood slathered his left hand and arm to the elbow, the right one lacerated and ensleeved with blood right to the shoulder. He looked to have gathered up some man's spilled wet insides and tried, by hand, to restore them to the voided cavity. Invisible yet bright, heatless but unbearably hot, he bore a corona any fool could feel. Xho Xho alone was unawed, hanging back from fear of the forest, not of the Sorcerer.

Demane knew them by turban, shaggy hair, narrow shoulders. Kazza, Wilfredo, Faried. He called. "I'ma do my best to meet up with you down south. Go on! Catch up with the caravan. I see you when the caravan cross that other stream southside of the Wildeeps, all right?"

Kazza crept a little closer. "You dead, Sorcerer? Come back some kind of haint?"

Demane chuckled. "No, baby." A grim noise, for a

chuckle. "I just made a bargain, became what y'all been calling me—a sorcerer. It ain't easy for me to get on the Road or leave the Wildeeps anymore." Demane put a hand back against the nearest trunk and leaned, taking seat at the roots. He rested his hands on updrawn knees. "I want to see Sea-john down in Great Olorum. Y'all go run after the caravan. I see you down at other end of the Wildeeps, *Godwilling*, as Faedou say. Take that jukiere head to show Master Suresh and them."

Xho Xho stepped into the forest. The rest cried out in alarm. The smeared apparition of the boy wobbled as if seen through rheum or tears, and became clear once off the Road, by the tree where Demane sat. "Faedou all of a sudden just up and fell out. You better come see, Sorcerer. He dying, I think." Xho Xho took hold of a filthy hand and tried to pull Demane to standing: budging him not. "And where's the captain?"

"I told you, little man," Demane said. "I cain't get onto the Road." On both cheeks he bore a delta of rinsed skin.

Willy called. "Ehtá a punto de morir, Sorcerer. I seen his leg, and it look about rotted off already. How he come this far on it, I don't even know. Tell you this, though. If you don't work some kind of sorcery on him *quick*, Faedou will be stone dead fore the night come."

Demane looked out onto the Road. Someone lay there stretched out on blankets just where the brothers had knelt. It was like peering down into deep running water, trying to see across the veil between the Road and Wildeeps. From here, he couldn't make out who lay there, or whether that brother stirred, or his chest still rose and fell.

Demane stood and wiped either eye with a wrist. "Let me see what I could do. Y'all carry him to me. The Wildeeps won't hurt none of you. This whole place is my house now." Afraid, the brothers dithered. Demane spoke again, in tones to get them jumping. "All right! Don't just stand there stupid! Bring him here." As they moved to obey Demane gave Xho Xho a little push back towards the others. "Help em carry, little man. You and Walead can lift one corner of the blankets together."

Like a son too often told before, *Be patient, your father's coming back soon*, Xho Xho clung to the Sorcerer's hand. "Wait. Tell me something, though," the boy said. "What happen to the captain?"

Demane might have answered, but a fit of palsy took his face. His mouth worked soundlessly. He shook his head.

The shroud of leaves frays and a brightness ahead dapples the jungle. There are glimpses of the jagged stump rising into sunlight. He can hear but not yet see the jook-toothed tiger growling, the captain and his harsh, controlled pants. All while Demane runs, he shouts too, I'm coming. Hang on. There was another one. I killed it. He bursts out into hot glare. Captain and the tiger are a hundred long paces up, tangling where other trees overshadow the compost of leaf and woodrot remaining of the felled tree's canopy. Captain has lost his spear and fights with a sword. It's always been sheathed across his back, although he but rarely draws it. A sword's very much the wrong weapon, requiring far too close quarters, for the power and claws of a jukiere. Captain's spear must have broken. He wouldn't just throw it aside, *he wouldn't*.

First one paw and then the other bats at him. As sails of a ship belly in the wind, when tacking hard off one course to another, Captain bows deeply over the claws, and as fast again, bows at a slightly altered angle. His robe's much slashed but person still unscathed. As if down some abyss in freefall, Captain drops. The tiger leaps over and misses pinning him flat. He's up off the ground, afoot when she wheels on him with chops snapping. He skips back blindly from the fangs and bringing around his sword twohanded, all his might in the blow, arrests the jukiere's whirling lunge. This lays another thin red stripe through the cat's darkbrindled fur. She flinches, though not much. That cut and the others are weirdly shallow. The wizard won't be killed without a better weapon than the one Captain holds . . . Demane should have been at his side all along. *Isa.* Hang on, Isa. Captain's attention splits for an instant. He must see Demane coming through the light and hear his shouts. That much he's almost sure of.

Demane turns an ankle in foul grease: Some meat-stuff or slick runoff, once a pig or man. He springs up and hobbles on. If delayed at all, it's half an instant, if hurt he's hardly slower than before: still, these charges will figure among those he tenders against himself on nights here-after, when once more sitting up in sleepless reverie. The man you could have saved if you'd gotten him sooner under your care lies struggling in his agonies. And *now*, only at the very end, he turns to your voice and chooses to trust. There you kneel and whisper, urging him toward the one choice life still offers. He takes it. There's a look to that, as grace suffuses a wracked visage. *Let go, Faedou. It's all right now. Let go.* Even the best of healers come to learn this look. It steals then over the captain's face. He quits his brilliant efforts and stops moving within easy reach of teeth and claws. The sword slips from his hand. Demane *shouts.* The distance is chancy, his throwing arm badly wounded, but still he hurls the spear.

About the Author

Kai Ashante Wilson's stories "Super Bass" and "The Devil in America," the latter of which was nominated for the Nebula, the Shirley Jackson, and the World Fantasy Awards, can be read online gratis at *Tor.com*. His story «*Légendaire.*» can be read in the anthology *Stories for Chip*, which celebrates the legacy of science fiction grandmaster Samuel R. Delany. Kai Ashante Wilson lives in New York City.

TOR·COM

Science fiction. Fantasy.
The universe.
And related subjects.

⁎

More than just a publisher's website, Tor.com
is a venue for **original fiction, comics,** and
discussion of the entire field of SF and fantasy,
in all media and from all sources. Visit our site
today—and join the conversation yourself.